WITHDRAWN

REDWOOD LIBRARY

NEWPORT, R. I.

THE HONEY BUNCH

A NOVEL

THE HONEY BUNCH

by PATRICIA ZELVER

An Atlantic Monthly Press Book
LITTLE, BROWN AND COMPANY
BOSTON · TORONTO

COPYRIGHT © 1969 BY PATRICIA ZELVER

ALL RIGHTS RESERVED. NO PART OF THIS BOOK MAY BE REPRO-
DUCED IN ANY FORM OR BY ANY ELECTRONIC OR MECHANICAL
MEANS INCLUDING INFORMATION STORAGE AND RETRIEVAL SYS-
TEMS WITHOUT PERMISSION IN WRITING FROM THE PUBLISHER,
EXCEPT BY A REVIEWER WHO MAY QUOTE BRIEF PASSAGES IN A
REVIEW.

LIBRARY OF CONGRESS CATALOG CARD NO. 78-97909

FIRST EDITION

ATLANTIC—LITTLE, BROWN BOOKS
ARE PUBLISHED BY
LITTLE, BROWN AND COMPANY
IN ASSOCIATION WITH
THE ATLANTIC MONTHLY PRESS

Published simultaneously in Canada
by Little, Brown & Company (Canada) Limited

PRINTED IN THE UNITED STATES OF AMERICA

To the memory of my parents

JAN 21 70

THE HONEY BUNCH

1

ON AN AFTERNOON in late May, 1965, the creative
writing class at Miss Parker's School for Girls in
Mill Valley, California — a group of three carefully selected young ladies — gathered in Miss Susanna Swope's sitting room. No other teacher at
the school had a sitting room; Susanna had simply
requisitioned it. Occasionally, the younger faculty
would get together and mutter about it; once, a
delegation even called upon the headmistress to
protest. They complained that the sitting room
gave Miss Swope too personal an influence over
her class. Did the headmistress know, for example,
that Miss Swope had a younger brother who had
served time in a penitentiary?

"Oh, yes, the brother," said the headmistress,
who had not known.

The younger faculty explained that they did not
hold this against Miss Swope; they were broad-
minded. They merely questioned her judgment in
telling such things to impressionable young girls.

The headmistress, who both disliked and feared

Susanna, told the delegation that Miss Swope was a tradition, and, though she sympathized with their position, it might be better to leave "well enough alone."

The younger faculty had picked up this phrase, and, privately, among themselves, referred to Miss Swope as Miss Well-Enough.

Susanna sat at the end of the long heavy Renaissance-style table and presided over the teapot. The teapot was a gleaming baroque silver vessel, which Susanna had wheedled out of Bennet Tidewater's mother, following his death. Each day, after teatime, she presented the pot to one of the girls to polish; this was considered to be an honor. Susanna would not permit tea bags, and had her own special brand of English tea; she poured hot water from a smaller silver pot into a thin china cup. She wore a beige wool dress. Her hair, once a straw-colored blonde, now flecked with gray, was wrapped about her long face in thick Germanic braids. Over the years, her features had grown larger; her manner, more decisive.

"When we last met we had just finished Bitsy's story," said Susanna, after the tea was served. "I believe you will recall the plot: the young hero who joined the Peace Corps rather than go into his father's brokerage firm, and, who, on the Amazon, meets the young native girl, who convinces him that her primitive way of life is better than the scientific and hygienic methods he is attempting to bring to her people. At the last, when he is dying, he reviews his life, and comes to the conclusion that the girl was right. Is that correct, Bitsy?"

Bitsy Collier nodded, shyly.

"Very well," said Susanna, "I shall now make a few comments — only a few — then open it up for class discussion. One thing comes to mind immediately. Your hero dies of a venereal disease, which he caught from the native girl. I am not questioning your premise that the primitive life he had discovered was better than that of his own country; it merely seems ironic that it was lack of hygiene that caused his death. And yet your story does not seem to be ironic. Does anyone remember the definition of irony?"

Barby Hall raised her hand. Susanna nodded.

"A kind of ridicule which exposes the faults of others, by seeming to adopt them."

"Excellent. I'm afraid, Bitsy, that this, in itself, invalidates your theme. Couldn't the young man die from some accident, perhaps caused by some of his industrial machinery? That, of course, is for the author to work out.

"Then, while he reviews his life, you say, I shall quote, 'Childhood? His mother? A vague, pretty woman in a black strapless evening gown.' Did she always wear a black strapless evening gown? If this is the way he remembers her, in his fevered mind, perhaps you might point this out. You might say, for example, 'He remembered her *best* in her black strapless evening gown,' or, 'Somehow, he could only see her —' et cetera.

"Then, further on, 'his father, that distant tycoon, enmeshed in the daily meanderings of the stock market.' Can one become enmeshed in meanderings? I do not think so.

"Proper accurate language is all that I can really teach you, and it seems that I am failing at that. However, I shall make some *suggestions,* considering subject matter. Please correct me, if I am wrong, Bitsy, but it is my *guess* that you are not intimately acquainted with the sort of experience or locale you have described. I appreciate the fact that you have been reading one of our master stylists, at your age you can't go wrong doing that, your style is not yet formed. But, surely, there is something in your young life that might capture your imagination. You live in Los Altos Hills; you have a mother and a father and, I believe, a horse or two. There is drama in everyday existence; you must learn to recognize it. Take myself, for example —"

Susanna stood up and took several steps about the room. The girls watched her, enraptured.

"As you all know, I grew up in a small provincial town in Oregon." She stopped and stood very still.

The girls nodded, eagerly.

"If I shut my eyes right this minute," said Susanna, shutting her eyes, "I can smell the pear blossoms in spring, the smoky air in autumn. I can see the Rialto Theatre. I can see the Natatorium, where we swam. I can see the Cozy Nook. I can see the McKittricks' living room in all its metamorphoses. I can see every detail of Bennet Tidewater's room." She opened her eyes and looked at the three girls, severely. "I am not an author, it was not given to me to be that, but I think I understand something about the importance of 'writing truly,' if I may quote from the gentleman whom Bitsy has been reading." Susanna sat down. "Has anyone anything to say?" she said.

There was a moment of silence. Then, "What are the symptoms of soft chancre?" said Barby Hall.

"That is an excellent question, and I would suggest, Barby, that, before our next session, you go to the library and look it up."

"Noble savage is a cliché," said Cathy Gregerson.

"I purposely let that go, hoping someone would catch it," said Susanna.

"What is the difference between truly lovemaking and untruly lovemaking?" Barby asked.

"Let us ask that of Bitsy," said Susanna.

"Perhaps I should have said 'nice,' " Bitsy said.

Susanna glanced at her watch. "We have only five minutes left, there is going to be an assembly this afternoon."

"Then tell us about Norton," said Barby.

"Please, please, tell us about Bennet Tidewater," Cathy said.

"Hand me the Notebook, please," said Susanna.

Bitsy ran to the bookshelf. "Volume I or Volume II?" she asked.

"Bennet Tidewater is only in Volume I," said Barby.

"He was killed in a barroom brawl," said Cathy.

"Murdered," corrected Susanna.

She opened Volume I, and turned the pages. "I shall just have time to read Bennet's vital statistics," she said.

Bennet Tidewater. Five feet, eleven and one-half inches, weight approximately 160 pounds. Brown eyes; brown, slightly curly hair; lithe and strong with cat-like grace. A rather precise, formal diction. Except on Sundays, when he dressed for church, he usually wore old pants and an old brown sweater. His manners were courtly and elaborate. He believed in Evil, and had a Tragic Sense of Life.

"Any questions?"

"He was homosexual, was he not, Miss Swope?" asked Barby.

"Undoubtedly," said Susanna.

"But he talked about getting married, didn't he?" said Bitsy.

"He desired a *mariage de convenance*. Do you know what that means?" Susanna said.

"I know," said Barby. "It's like, well, the French, in the old days, you married someone your family told you to, for money or land or an old name or —"

"In Bennet's case, he wanted to marry a girl with a strong chin in order to strengthen the Tidewater chin, which was weak," Susanna said. "Gather up your things, girls, there is the bell. Cathy, I believe it is your turn to polish the teapot."

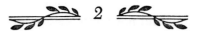 2

JANET KRONER, who had been Janet Springer, had lived in San Francisco ever since the end of World War II, but she still subscribed to the *Norton News Sentinel,* back copies of which she kept stacked in a storage closet for six months at a time. She considered this fact shameful; she had not even had the courage to tell Dr. Kedy about it. It was in this newspaper, in the Locals and Personals (not even on the society page), which was filled with new names which Janet did not know — she had not been back to Norton, herself, for almost fifteen years — that she read about Miss Susanna Swope's approaching visit to Norton.

Mrs. Muriel Swope of the Hilltop Senior Citizens Home is expecting her daughter, Miss Susanna Swope, at the end of the week for a short visit before she leaves for Europe, where she will chaperone a group of girls on a Tour. Miss Swope is a teacher at Miss Parker's School for Girls in Mill Valley, California. She is a graduate of Norton High School, and attended the University of Oregon.

It is the end of an era, thought Janet. The treachery of the enterprise made her go weak all over. Susanna did not go to Norton without letting her know. This was a sort of Natural Law, a custom formed by Time; to break it would be a subtle, unmentionable, yet utterly blatant betrayal.

But perhaps Susanna would call, after all. It was now only Tuesday, Janet reassured herself.

She knew she tended toward hysteria; Dr. Kedy had told her so.

But by late Wednesday, she could no longer suppress her panic. For by now she had made her plan, and Susanna was necessary to it. The plan seemed so absolutely right, even Dr. Kedy couldn't object. Still, Dr. Kedy was unpredictable. Janet was not sorry this lady was out of town for two weeks. When she returned, she would confront her with a "fait accompli."

Was it possible that Susanna would not call at all? She knew it was a possibility. Recently Susanna would sometimes wait an entire week upon returning from Norton before phoning Janet, and, as if this were not bad enough, would feign an Olympian detachment about the latest "gossip," so that Janet had to force it out of her by stratagems. Any show of eagerness on her part delayed the process.

Janet sat down at the curious little art nouveau desk — it had been a lucky "find" on McAllister Street. She lit a cigarette, then idly thumbed through her address book. Of course, she knew Susanna's number by heart; but she was playing for time. Perhaps she would call up some friends, a married couple or two and a single man, and put a little party together instead.

— Barry Aldridge, a photographer, she had met him at a gallery opening a few weeks ago; he had phoned her twice. He was not uninteresting. Still the number of ex-wives he had collected frightened her: at her age, she was used to one or two, but four seemed excessive.

— Marty Brown, architect. One wife, but five children.

— Rod Clement, fifty, and never married at all. This could be even scarier.

". . . *is expecting her daughter at the end of the week.*" Susanna was not only treacherous, she was sadistic. Still, she had to know. Sighing at her own weakness, she closed the little book, and dialed the number of the Parker School.

3

"TELL US about Gerald Kroner," said Barby to Susanna.

"I met him only once, over cocktails, in Janet's apartment. It was in 1956. They had been married for a week. He was in the textile business, and supposedly rich."

"Was he handsome?" said Bitsy.

"If you will hand me Volume II, please," said Susanna.

She opened it at "Gerald Kroner," and began to read:

Tall, like Janet. Thin. Blond-red hair. Very white skin. Very blue eyes. Perhaps thirty-five. Did he have a mustache? I have the impression that he did, but now I am not certain. Can I ask Janet? I do not think I can. Wears a ring. On the telephone Janet told me he is an intellectual and speaks three languages. Last evening he spoke only English. He mixed our drinks meticulously, but did not drink himself.

Susanna glanced up. "Perhaps he belonged to a religion or had a stomach ulcer, or had been an alcoholic. Excluding these possibilities, I wonder if you can trust a man who does not drink."

I asked him where his home was. He replied, "Where I hang my hat." I wonder if you can trust a man who gives such a reply. He is at present hanging his hat in Janet's apartment.

She closed the notebook. "He hung it there for a month," she said.

"And then they were divorced?" said Cathy.

"And you lied in the testimony and said he had beaten Janet," Barby said.

"Yes."

"Didn't that embarrass you in front of Gerald Kroner?"

"Gerald Kroner was not present. He did not contest the divorce. There was no property settlement, because, it seemed, he had no property after all."

"What do you think really happened, Miss Swope?" said Cathy.

"Perhaps he did not appreciate her good bony structure," said Bitsy.

"When people get married they draw down a blind and one never really knows what goes on behind it. Janet told me they were sexually incompatible, whatever that may mean. Does anyone know what being sexually incompatible is?"

"I thought it meant when the man can't do it," Cathy said.

"Say what you mean, say 'when the man can't have sexual intercourse,'" said Susanna.

"Yes, I thought that's what it meant."

"I should think that would certainly fall under the heading of Sexual Incompatibility. But perhaps it is other things, too."

"Sometimes at first they are nervous," Barby said.

"A good shot of whiskey is said to help," said Bitsy.

"But Gerald Kroner did not drink," said Cathy.

"Perhaps he was a homosexual," Barby said.

"Like Bennet Tidewater," said Cathy.

"He was not like Bennet Tidewater, not in the least," said Susanna.

"Perhaps he had a social disease," said Barby.

"There is the telephone," said Susanna. "Cathy, will you answer it, please?"

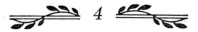

4

ONE WOULD NOT HAVE THOUGHT, looking at Janet that she was obsessed by fears of betrayal. Her appearance gave the opposite impression — that of poise, self-confidence, even serenity. She was tall and very fair and very elegant in her good white silk blouse and good tweed skirt and good, very high-heeled shoes — a costume designed to reveal her aristocratic bony structure. She wore three slender antique gold bracelets on one arm, and tiny gold loops in her ears. Any woman would know that, at forty-two, she could not have such straight, shining, blonde hair without assistance, yet the job had been done so well, in the best shop, that it looked natural. There was almost, but not quite, an air of breeding about Janet; a something faintly "English" and "country"; one might have guessed she had attended a good girls' private school in the East, somewhere, instead of Norton High — unless, perhaps, one was a graduate of such a school oneself.

The room in which she sat in her Russian Hill apartment was subdued and elegant, too; old, worn, thin, Oriental rugs covered the dark polished floors; there was a good modern couch, a Japanese tansu, the art nouveau desk, old prints in gold leaf frames upon the white walls. On the wall above her desk hung faded family portraits in old walnut frames — a photograph of her father, as a child, playing ice hockey in knickers; a photograph of her mother in a beaver coat and muff. Janet was without any family, now, and the pictures were intended to give an extra dimension, a depth to the image she hoped to provoke from the room.

On the coffee table were copies of *Réalités*, *Interiors* and *California Arts and Architecture*. Books, too, added a certain "note." There were new novels and collections of verse; she made it a point to buy the books of poets who came to read at the Poetry Center, though she never seemed to have the time to go to hear them. In her bookshelf were the old leather-bound editions of Shakespeare and Browning which had belonged to her mother.

The apartment was not at all like Norton, or Mrs. McKittrick's avocado greens and luggage tans. She had only to gaze out of her window to be reminded of this. What was extraordinary about it was the view it offered. She looked out upon the City, upon the hills, crowded with white buildings, upon the Bay and the Bay Bridge, upon Alcatraz Island and ships, the Ferry Building, the Shell Building, and a vast stretch of sky, which often contained a jet plane or a tiny helicopter, ready to land. The room had been described by one of her colleagues as a "small gem," set on the side of a hill.

Indeed, if there were anything wrong with the room, it was this air of contrivance, which Janet, for all her skill, had not quite managed to conceal. There was still a touch of the decorator, as though someone had stood, appraisingly, in the empty room, had held a notebook and pencil, and looked about with narrowed eyes, one finger upon her chin; had then taken several steps backwards and looked again. One had the feeling that, at any moment, the tansu or the art nouveau desk would vanish; that these supposedly "old things" of hers would journey into other people's homes, to be re-

placed by equally interesting "pieces." This uneasiness seemed even to extend to the family portraits; there was a sense of impermanence, despite
the artful air.

For the fact was, Janet was a decorator. She
sold "Good Taste," which, in itself, she felt to be
vulgar. Well-bred people, she supposed, never cal-
culated effects in this way; they never hunted in
junk stores for "finds," or worried over color
schemes. They simply surrounded themselves with
the things they somehow already possessed. Or, if
they used Janet, as many of them did, they would
often say, "That's nice," to her suggestions, in a
way which made her imagine there were other,
more important matters upon their minds.

Janet was as frightened by vulgarity as she was
by betrayal. But what could she do? This was her
one, small talent; she had built up a loyal clientele,
and it provided a good income. She ought to be
proud of herself, of her talent; Dr. Kedy had said
so. She sat, ankles crossed, back straight, inhaling
her cigarette, and waited for someone to answer at
Susanna's school.

"Miss Parker's," a young voice said.
"I wonder if I might please speak to Miss Susanna Swope?"

There were subdued school noises in the background, then, at last, Susanna's crisp voice.

"Susanna, this is Jan."

"Oh, Jan, how are you?"

"I'm fine, dear, do you have time to chat, or is this a bad time?"

"There's never any perfect time over here," said Susanna, "so this will do nicely. Is there anything special?"

"Yes, as a matter of fact, there is. I have to go to Norton, some business, that piece of land I inherited from my parents, and I wondered if there's the slightest chance you could come, too? We could all have a Reunion, you and Honey and me. Heaven knows, it's about time the Trio got together."

"What an odd coincidence, I was going to call you," Susanna said.

"So, you planned all this, knowing I would be away," Dr. Kedy would say, in her crisp, cold, professional woman's voice.

"Yes, I admit it!"

"Well, how did it go? Did you see Joseph?"

"No." This was the surprise she had for Dr. Kedy. She could go to Norton and not see Joseph, at least not see him alone. This would be her triumph. She felt utterly confident, so confident, in fact, that she was not even going to pack what she cynically called her Fallen Woman's Wardrobe. No seductive lingerie, not even a nightgown. She would go to Norton and have a nice Reunion luncheon, just like the mature, normal, well-balanced person she now was, and, afterwards, how splendid and proud she would feel, telling Dr. Kedy about it.

She would not see Joseph. And why should she, since she didn't even like him, she had discovered? Why should she bother to see someone she didn't even like? There had been, after all, other men in her life since her divorce. Joseph was not the first. When she thought of it, she could not help but wonder what Honey had ever seen in him?

"Now, do I win a gold star, Dr. Kedy? Don't you think my behavior was admirable?"

"What do you think?" Dr. Kedy would say.

And Janet would answer, calmly, simply, "I think it was."

"That's what matters, what *you* think," Dr. Kedy would say.

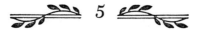

5

WHEN SUSANNA RETURNED to her room that evening, she took down Volume II of the Norton Note-books, and opened it in the middle, where the pages were blank, and began to write, in her pre-cise, cramped hand.

A Plot Afoot

Janet Kroner, née Springer, telephoned me at 7:35 P.M. June 2nd, to suggest that I accompany her to Norton, and that she and Honey and I hold a Reunion at luncheon at the Country Club. She will stay at the Hotel Jackson. Poor Janet.

Later that year, when she read this entry to a group of her students, one of them asked, "Why did you say, 'Poor Janet'? You didn't know what was going to happen, did you?"

"Of course I didn't know," said Susanna. "I wrote 'Poor Janet' because she sounded so pa-thetic, somehow, on the telephone, as if holding a

Reunion would somehow break the awful Norton Spell she was under — would, somehow, turn her into the fine, splendid person we all long to be."

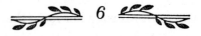

6

THERE WERE TWO MYSTERIES about his wife that Joseph Porter had never fathomed, and these were the two things about her that drove him wild.

The first was her Catholicism. Honey had joined the Church, of all things, *after* their marriage, and for no discernible, outward, emotional reason; there had been no sudden revelation, no apparent soul-searching; she had simply, one day, gone down and signed up for Instruction and become confirmed. When he asked her, shyly, what had brought it on, she said simply that she had often considered it, and had, at last, made up her mind. Nor was she, like so many converts, any more zealous a Catholic than one born into the faith. She was not the sort who is drawn to the Church by love of the exotic or the need for ritual, either. Her personality, except for a certain frivolity, was almost Quaker in its simplicity; she never sought

dramatic effects. She accepted her new religion serenely, as she accepted everything else. Sometimes
he thought it was this serenity that disturbed him
most of all.

On top of all this, she had never attempted in
any way he could see to proselytize their daughters, now age ten and eleven, who had been born
before her conversion. Which made it very difficult
for him to understand why, in hell's sakes, she had
turned Catholic?

He had, of course, discussed this with Janet the
next time he went to San Francisco; perhaps he
had gone there on purpose to discuss it with her.
Honey's conversion had acted upon their wavering
affair in much the same way the discovery that
Honey had a lover might have done; though both
had sworn to terminate the affair, they had sought
each other out, to share and ponder together this
new event.

"It must be us, she must know," said Janet.

"I have never told her," said Joseph. He was too
honorable to consider purging his own guilt at his
wife's expense.

"She may have found out. It might be a kind of
revenge."

"Honey isn't revengeful. She doesn't plot."

"Well, then, I may as well say it. It's Bennet
Tidewater."

"You mean, that fairy?"

Janet nodded.

Joseph groaned. "Sometimes I think all of you are nuts," he said. "I mean, all of you Trio. Look at Susanna. She's pretty eccentric. Frankly, she gives me the creeps, sometimes. I get the feeling she's putting everything down in a notebook. And Honey is, well, different. And now you tell me calmly that Bennet Tidewater is responsible for her conversion. I never knew this Bennet Tidewater, I am relieved to say, but for God's sakes, he's been dead for years."

"He was considering becoming Catholic before he died," said Janet.

"I can't stand it, it doesn't make any sense," Joseph cried. "Of course," he added, after a moment, "it doesn't make any sense about us, either. What am I doing here, in your apartment?"

"You are seeking your wife," said Janet, bitterly. "And I am a member of the Trio."

"You are very kind and patient and lovely," Joseph said. He put his arm about her. "To hell with the Trio," he said, "let me fix us a drink."

They had had the drink, and then another, and then they had made love. Both thought it was for the last time.

After all, thought Joseph, later, I'm not even her type. She knows other more sophisticated, arty guys. Architects. Artists. She didn't need to fool around with a small-town, Oregon lumberman, who comes to San Franciso on business.

"Seeking his wife."

The second mystery was Honey's Past. Joseph had not known her in this glorious time of her youth; he had met her when he was stationed at Camp Jackson, outside of Norton, and Honey was a pretty, frivolous widow, who went out with a different officer every night. She was now plump and matronly in a nice, soft, attractive way; one would have guessed she had been a pretty girl. But, good Lord, thought Joseph, there have always been pretty girls who grow into nice attractive women; there were even girls not so pretty who grew into women, like Janet, who were not plump and matronly at all, and who wore their clothes with more chic. Why was he, Joseph, plagued by this legendary beauty, a beauty which, evidently he had never possessed, and never would, this was made plain by both her attitude and that of others.

Not that Honey was in any way proud, or stand-offish, or someone who lived in the Past. That he could have handled, he could have mocked and teased. No, it was something more subtle, and harder to deal with.

Someone would say something. Susanna, on one

of her visits — "that was after Honey became
beautiful —" She would say this as one might cas-
ually mention any historical epoch, as one might
say, "that was after the War."

Or, his mad mother-in-law. "You should have
been at her wedding, Joseph."

"I was at her wedding, Mother."

"Oh, I don't mean that one. That one was nothing compared to the first. I decorated the church
in gold and green. The only white note was the
bride. People gasped when she came down the
aisle."

Or Congressman Richard "Buzzy" Heffelfinger.
"Remember the night after the prom when we
drove off with Arthur and didn't know it?"

And Honey and the Congressman would go into
fits of secret, wild laughter.

Then Buzzy would say, "Arthur was the Mc-
Kittricks' dog. He loved to ride in cars."

But Joseph could never quite see what was all
that funny about that particular occurrence.

"You should have seen Honey that night," Buzzy
said to Joseph. "She looked like Brenda Diana Duff
Frazier. Remember, that debutante in all the
ads?"

Though the Congressman's eyes were now sight-
less, he had once seen what Joseph would never
see — his wife at the time of her glory. To be envi-

ous of a blind man was another burden which Joseph had to bear.

Honey, who was modest in every other way, would accept these compliments calmly, as if they really were not compliments at all, but ordinary statements of fact. Nevertheless, it was undoubtedly a special sort of fact, for Joseph saw what happened in her eyes. Her eyes were large and long-lashed and deep blue, still the eyes of that young girl whom he sometimes wished had never existed. And these eyes would change. They would become, briefly, dreamy and surprised, as if she suddenly looked upon and marveled at that extraordinary creature who was Honey McKittrick in her teens. And he would grow wild and frenzied with jealousy. He could not help it.

And it was happening, now. They were sitting at the breakfast table and Honey was reading a letter she had just opened. He could see it suddenly happening, as she put the letter down, and looked up at him, but not really at him, at something else which was not within his vision.

"What is it?" he said, defensively, on guard.

"Janet and Susanna are coming. They want a Reunion."

Joseph felt suddenly sick and trapped. After a moment he managed to say, "A Reunion? Whose idea was that?"

"The letter is from Janet, poor dear. She's had such a disappointing life." Honey smiled at him, across the table. "As she points out, the three of us haven't been together for ages. After all, we were known as the Trio." She smiled. "Why, I don't think I've seen Janet since her mother died, and she came up for the funeral. That must have been fifteen years ago."

"You could have," said Joseph. "I've invited you to San Francisco often enough."

"I know, dear. I wish I could have come. But, as Janet says, the Trio will be together at last."

"The Trio," said Joseph. "You're not the Trio, now. You're a married woman."

"Sometimes I think you're jealous of us," Honey said, gaily. She rose from the table and gave Joseph a kiss upon his cheek. "It's late, you know. I have to get Susie and Jan off to school. And I must remember to make a reservation for lunch at the club. It will be nice to see Janet and Susanna both at once. But isn't it a pity Bennet Tidewater can't be here, too?"

"I don't understand how you proper, nicely brought-up ladies could want to be with someone who was murdered in a fairy brawl," Joseph said. "But, then, I suppose there's a lot I don't understand," he added wryly.

"No one expects you to, dearest," said Honey.

And no one did, thought Joseph. Not Honey, not eccentric Susanna, not even Janet. They humored him, oddly, as if he were a pet dog.

"I better go too. I'm flying up to Jackson Falls this afternoon, so I'll be home late."

"Don't forget, you promised to take the girls up this weekend. They've been talking about it."

"I haven't forgotten," said Joseph, who was a good father. "We'll go to Possum Bridge. They've put in a new landing strip." He rose, and bent over her and she automatically turned her cheek for his kiss. "Why don't you plan to come with us?" he said.

"Oh dearest, you know how nervous I get, having to fly."

"All right," he said. In the morning sunlight, her hair looked quite gray. This observation made him feel suddenly closer to her.

"Your hair's turning gray," he said affectionately.

She smiled. "I suppose I could do something about it, but it seems like such a bother."

"I like it this way."

"That's what Buzzy said."

"Buzzy? But he can't see it!"

"Oh, I told him about it," said Honey.

7

NORTON WAS DIVIDED into two districts: the Hill,
which was fashionable, and the rest of the town,
which was not. The Hill was not so much a hill as a
rising slope, and the first homes were built on the
beginning of the rise, close to town. Later, after
the Country Club was built in 1927, this part of
the Hill was known as the Lower Hill; much later,
during Mrs. McKittrick's dotage, many of the
Lower Slope homes were turned into apartment
houses, rest homes, and offices.

When Honey was born, the McKittricks bought
the old Bamford house on the Lower Hill, which
was then just called the Hill. It was the sort of old,
sprawling, slightly ramshackle house one might
buy for a growing family. But the McKittrick family did not grow. Mrs. McKittrick did not believe
in people multiplying "like rabbits," as she used to
say. One very precious little girl was quite enough;
the good God had granted her all that she desired;
Dr. McKittrick had had no choice but to agree.

Nor did the old Bamford house remain ramshackle, or even the "old Bamford house" for long. Mrs. McKittrick was small and pretty and rather frail and suffered from nerves; but she had what she called "drive."

"I have drive," she used to say. "There's one thing you can say about me, when I want something done, I have a one-track mind."

She believed in Charm and Personality as firmly as others have believed in Courage and Fortitude, and she soon bestowed these attributes upon her house. Her Bible was *House and Garden* and *House Beautiful*.

"My Bible is *House and Garden* and *House Beautiful*," she used to say. "They are my Scriptures. I suppose that sounds sacrilegious, perhaps it is."

She saved clippings from these magazines in cardboard boxes, and, over the years, the interior of her house changed constantly, depending upon what the Scriptures dictated.

She haunted junk stores and auctions, and was proud of the fact that few of her possessions were bought new.

"Anyone can walk into Gidol's Furniture Store and say, 'I'll take that,'" she used to say. "But that wouldn't do for me, at all. I like to express my own Personality."

If the Doctor complained of her extravagance,

she would point out that her finds would increase in value — "It's like having money in the bank."

At various times her kitchen was Pennsylvania Dutch; the dining room, Early American; the Living Room, Monterey-Spanish; the master bedroom, French Provincial; the sun-room, which she had renamed The Lanai, Hawaiian. She had done Honey's room from an article, "How to Decorate for Your Teen-age Daughter." Dotted swiss curtains covered the windows; Godey prints hung on the wall; there was a kidney-shaped dressing table, covered with an eyelet embroidery flounce, and a bench, with a similar flounce, in front of it.

Later, in her decadent period, the atmospheric effects were largely what Bennet Tidewater called Victorian Whorehouse.

"I see we have more money in the bank," the Doctor would say, when he was confronted by a new antique, or freshly hung wallpaper.

Mrs. McKittrick was an indoor type of lady, and confined her activities mostly to the interior. Outside, the house had an unkempt, lackadaisical air. It was surrounded, in front, by a large, weed-choked lawn, and dotted with oak trees. Many years later, in her dotage, she put up an iron fence which she salvaged from the old courthouse when it was torn down. The gate to the fence had pikes on it, the sort one sticks one's enemies' heads on as a warn-

ing to the rest of the populace. But, in the days
when Honey was growing up, there was no gate,
and friends of the McKittricks wore a path across
the lawn, taking a shortcut from the sidewalk to
the porch.

There was also a large yard in the back. In the
center of this yard was a rectangular swimming
tank, which, with its utilitarian, functional lines —
unlandscaped, and smelling of chlorine — resem-
bled a miniature public reservoir. The swimming
tank represented Dr. McKittrick's sole revolt
against his wife's romantic tastes. She had not
wanted a pool; she considered it both dangerous
and vulgar. The vulgarity of it was confirmed in
her mind by the Doctor's swimming habits. Every
morning, except in the deep of winter, Dr. McKittrick swam "au naturel." He was not Spartan; he
was not a health fiend; he simply enjoyed swimming without his "gear."

Not once, during their entire married life, did
Mrs. McKittrick resign herself to this indecency.
She was of the opinion, opposed to that of more
ancient cultures, that the male organs should be
covered; that only little girls, who were built like
dolls, should be allowed to run around nude.

Mrs. McKittrick used the pool, once, herself. On
a hot Fourth of July, urged on by her family, fortified by a rum and cola, she entered the water, exe-

cuted a funny, old-fashioned breaststroke across the width and back, and then climbed out. She made no pronouncements; she simply never went in again. This became known as the time "Mother went swimming."

Mrs. McKittrick's attitude toward the pool did not stop it from being patronized, however; for a long time it was the only private pool in Norton. If you sink a washtub in the backyard, life will grow up around it. The McKittrick pool became a focus point for friends and friends of friends. It bred, in fact, an entire culture.

Mrs. McKittrick would have preferred more formal entertaining, but, finding she could not buck the tide, acquiesced. She would ask people, "Do you like swimming?" as if it were a strange and foreign taste. When Honey was in high school, she had the pool landscaped, and placed tables with umbrellas and ice cream chairs about it. She read articles entitled, "Entertaining Around Your Pool," and produced lavish barbecues — trays of hot hors d'oeuvres, fried chicken, sliced ham and cold drinks — which she brought to the poolside, almost as if she hoped by these embellishments to make it more respectable.

Mrs. McKittrick's two interests in life were her house and her family. The family came first, while Honey was growing up. Afterwards she fell back

upon the house, which, in the long run, proved
more reliable.

Dr. McKittrick was a large, rumpled, gentle
man, whose wrinkled suits were always sprinkled
with cigarette ash. He was not an especially talented doctor, but his kindness made up for this.
His patients, even when misdiagnosed, were loyal.
He never pressed a bill from rich or poor, and both
took advantage of him. His occasional investments
turned out badly, and no money was ever saved,
for both his wife and daughter were extravagant.
Nevertheless, they lived comfortably on his earn-
ings.

They had a series of girls from the country who
worked for low wages in order to live in town.
They had a Japanese gardener, Harry Nakamura,
from Norton's only non-Caucasian family. They
had a spaniel named Arthur, who lived to be
thirteen, and who, in 1939, was six years old.

The Swopes lived on one side of the McKittricks
in an English Tudor, and the Tidewaters on the
other side, in a cube-shaped, two-story house with
a peeling exterior, which Bennett called "Neo-
Nothing."

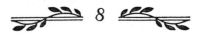

THE SPRINGERS did not live on the Hill; they had come down in the world. Janet Springer only knew this from being told; she had never seen them "up." She learned early, however, to recognize the signs of their fading distinction.

One of the signs was the six gnarled pear trees in their front yard. The trees, which now produced only bitter, stunted fruit, had once been a part of the Springer Orchard, which had existed before the Hill had become the fashionable place to live.

Then there was Mr. Springer, himself. He had a "Harvard accent," and elegant, formal manners, which he practiced democratically on both acquaintances and strangers alike. He would dazzle itinerant salesmen who came to the door to sell him something which he had no means to buy; tradesmen would hesitate asking him to pay his bills because it seemed wrong to trouble such a fine gentleman with vulgarities. He never just made a telephone call; it was always a ceremonious occasion. When the operator said, "Number please," Mr. Springer did not merely supply her with the number. Instead, he would say, "Good morning, this is Edwin Springer. I wonder if you could ring four-eight-two-five, please. Thank you so much."

He was the same at home with his family. Mundane, even, at times, sordid domestic problems, did not concern him. His wife attended to them, when they were attended to at all. If his manners masked a certain distant quality — a removed air — they remained exquisite in themselves — a work of art which graced a home that was, as Mrs. Springer liked to say, "barren of material beauty." She made this seem a virtue.

Mr. Springer had come from Massachusetts, where his family had had enough money to send him to Harvard for two years. After this he had gone to War, and had won a medal for bravery — assisting wounded soldiers under fire, while he, himself, had an enemy bullet in his shoulder. In 1920, he had come to Norton, to participate in the Orchard Boom, hoping, thereby, to fulfill his dream of living like a country gentleman. But the Boom had collapsed; his orchard had failed, and he had been forced to sell off all the land except the acre which contained the old two-story, clapboard farmhouse.

The Emerson Grade School had been built on

part of the old Springer orchard. Janet grew up in the shadow of this grim public structure, which looked like a brick prison. She attended it, and felt a stranger there. Later, when she read stories of English noblemen whose stately ancestral homes had been turned into hotels, she understood how they must have felt.

When Mr. Springer lost his money, he did what so many impoverished gentlemen who lack special training do; he went into Real Estate. Despite his social charm, he was not successful. As they grew poorer, his accent grew stronger, his manners more elaborate; his sole real interest became his never-to-be-completed book, *The History of Norton County.*

The History of Norton County was a ledger, containing the names of Norton County's pioneer families, the building of the railroad, the building of the bridge over Cold Creek, a list of Place Names, an account of two fires and three floods and various other freakish weather conditions, and a few pages of miscellaneous information, which he obtained by talking to whoever dropped into his office. He infuriated Mrs. McKittrick by referring to her home as the "old Bamford place."

When Mrs. Springer was going through Mr. Springer's effects, after he shot himself on top of

Little Butte one winter's afternoon, she found the History, and sent it to Janet, in San Francisco, with the following note.

If only your dear father might have finished his life's work, some of my sorrow might have been appeased. But it was not to be. His truly aristocratic nature kept him from intruding on the private lives of others — a courtesy which the great writers of history did not practice. For example, he could never bring himself to include a full account of the lurid Bigham Murder Case, because this would have meant interviewing Cap Bigham in jail. It often was said to him that this would not have stopped Gibbon or Macaulay, but his delicacy and refinement stood in his way.

Mrs. Springer, herself, contributed to the Springer distinction. Though she dressed shabbily and was no beauty, she was proud of what she called her "good bones."

"Yes, Honey is pretty, no doubt," she would say to Janet. "But that sort of prettiness does not hold up."

To Mrs. Springer, skeletons were more important than flesh; they had a permanence that lasted beyond the grave.

Voice quality was also important. Mrs. Springer had once taken elocution lessons at State Teacher's College. An elocutionary tone revealed a cultured mind. When the orchard failed, she went to work as a substitute teacher at Norton High. But it was always evident she was no ordinary teacher. Her grand manner and refined voice set her off from her colleagues.

The Springer house, barren of fine furnishings, contained leather-bound volumes of the English poets; their cats were named Laertes, Macbeth and Desdemona. She had organized the local Stratford Club, a ladies' organization devoted to reading the works of the Bard of Avon, aloud, under her tutelage. When Janet was very young, she was taught to recite:

> *The quality of mercy is not strain'd,*
> *It droppeth as the gentle rain from heaven*
> *Upon the place beneath; it is twice blest;*
> *It blesseth him that gives, and him that takes.*

She also sent Janet to the Episcopal Church so that she would become acquainted with the Book of Common Prayer.

Mrs. Springer believed that, if one were exposed early to divine meters, one could overlook the humiliation of wearing hand-me-down clothing from

richer friends' children, of riding in ancient auto-
mobiles and eating humble fare.

For it did not matter if you were poor, or plain
or awkward and too tall, if you spoke the "King's
English," and had a good bony structure.

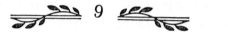

9

THE SWOPES lived next door to the McKittricks. Dr.
McKittrick was the Swope's family physician; Dr.
Swope attended to the McKittricks' teeth. At
Christmas time, they exchanged homemade cook-
ies. Apart from this, their only association was
Susanna's friendship with Honey. Mrs. McKittrick
found the Swopes lacking in social charm.

Dr. Swope was Norton's leading dentist. He was
a tall, angular, graceless man. There was an uncer-
tain air about everything he did; his movements
were neither positive nor professional. He puttered
about inside mouths in a seemingly aimless fashion, until, it seemed somehow by accident, the job
was done, surprising him as much as his patients.

To make up for this, he tried to provide entertainment which took the form of jokes and puns which he assiduously collected for this purpose, and which he delivered in a running monologue, in a dry, monotonous voice. He also employed foreign accents. He would be, perhaps, a Mexican. "Open mouth pleeze." Or, a Frenchman: "Speet out, Mademoiselle, see vu play." Or a German: "Danke, fraulein." One had the notion he was aware of the poverty of his material, and that this drove him on to desperate attempts to improve it.

He was seldom at home. He spent most of his free time at the Elks Club, playing pinochle, or attending meetings of the Masons, who met in their lodge above Buster Brown's.

His wife, Muriel, was in every way, his opposite. She was large, brisk, commanding and energetic. She had been at various times the president of the local chapter of the D.A.R., the chairman of the Norton Garden Club, the conductress of the Eastern Star, not to mention other more minor offices and distinctions. She was always marching, speaking, officiating and organizing, and, as a result, was seldom at home.

They had two children, Susanna, and a brother, Roger, who was four years younger, making him twelve in 1939.

Roger was a sullen, pimply boy who kept his own counsel. He had no friends, and every day, after school, he would go to his father's office and sit in the waiting room and read *The Elks Magazine* and *Collier's;* then, his pockets full of paper clips and rubber bands from the reception desk, he would stroll home, where usually Susanna waited with his supper. On Saturdays he went to the Rialto Theatre, where they showed gangster and cowboy movies, to study how to become a crook.

Susanna was lean and brown like a boy; her quietness hid a controlled energy. She had a tough, orphaned air, an occasional, swift smile, and never spoke to adults unless spoken to. When she was very young she learned, out of necessity, to cook and wash and iron and care for herself and Roger. For society, she went to the McKittricks.

"You could set Susanna down in Shanghai or Cairo and she would manage," Dr. McKittrick used to say, admiringly.

But Mrs. McKittrick would complain that Susanna gave her the creeps. She could never tell, for example, when she was in the house; she would enter the living room, assuming she was alone, and be startled half out of her wits to find Susanna sitting in an armchair, reading.

"Just sitting there, all alone, it's spooky, but, of course, the poor child has no home of her own. Her parents should never have had children!"

When she was young, Susanna used to steal. She

especially enjoyed stealing small items from the McKittricks, who she thought never noticed. She swiped a small silver ashtray and packages of Dr. McKittrick's Camels, and a book on wild flowers from the McKittrick living room. She pocketed a bracelet and a small ceramic horse from Honey's room; from Dr. and Mrs. McKittrick's bedroom she took seventy-five cents and a pair of gold studs and a jeweled Sigma Chi fraternity pin. Her grandest prize was an entire chocolate cake which she lifted from the McKittrick kitchen one day, having found a way to enter the house by raising the back door latch with a stick when no one was home. Arthur, the McKittricks' dog, was blamed for the theft; she served the cake to Roger, who asked no questions.

Susanna gave up stealing when she was thirteen and began to menstruate. But she held on to her loot, which was cached in a shoe box in her closet, the way one stores away mementos of one's youth.

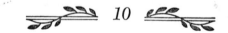

10

DR. MCKITTRICK had been brought up Catholic, but had fallen away from the Church before his marriage. Mrs. McKittrick had been brought up Congregationalist in Portland; there being no Congregationalist Church in Norton, she attended none at all. Mr. Springer had been a Unitarian; Mrs. Springer was an Episcopalian, and Mr. Springer attended services with her on Easter and Christmas time. Dr. Swope had been brought up Baptist, but the Masons now satisfied his spiritual needs. Mrs. Swope had been brought up Methodist, and still attended the church, where she was active in Women's Auxiliary.

Janet and Honey and Susanna had been confirmed in St. Matthew's Episcopal Church. They had been in the same confirmation class, whose motto, given to them by the bishop, was "Stir up the gift."

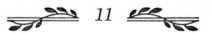

11

HONEY AND JANET AND SUSANNA were known to others, as well as themselves, as the Trio. Any falling out between any two of them was resolved privately; even mothers got nowhere if they attempted, as they sometimes did, to undermine the threesome.

By age sixteen the Trio had come to be an inde-
structible entity, a separate fourth body, apart
from their individual selves, to which they owed
allegiance and devotion, and in which they took
great pride.

Parents, teachers and friends sensed and re-
spected this. The Trio was a rare achievement, a
victory of discipline and idealism over irrational
forces. They were, each one of them, stronger for
having created it.

The Trio was a kind of Leisure Class. They had
neither the chores of the poor nor the duties and
disciplines of the rich. They could explore aspects
of existence that other, more Time-ridden people
were forced to ignore. They took up Feminism, the
Single Tax, Christian Science, White Slavery and
Present-Day Sexual Mores. They went on diets,
took sunbaths, practiced posture exercises and
read etiquette books and self-help articles for teen-
agers in the ladies magazines.

"When you enter a room, say to yourself, 'I am a
Queen, walking among my subjects.'"

"Just before you go out on a date, treat yourself
to an Upside-Down Facial. Stand on your head for
one minute and let the blood run to your face. This
will produce a pretty, blooming effect."

"Find out your parents' hobbies and take a
sympathetic interest in their problems. Learn their

little quirks and humor them. You will be surprised to learn that they are people, made of flesh and blood, just like you."

Janet began a series of exercises from the *Woman's Home Companion*, which promised to transform your figure within weeks, and increase your mental capabilities.

Susanna began the Bible and got as far as Kings.

Honey made a pet out of a poor girl named Evajean Treece.

All of this was Discipline to help them to improve their personalities.

"Think of yourself as a musical instrument in need of tuning," said Janet. "Say you are a piano that can only play loudly. Now, hit the keys ever so lightly and note the difference."

"Practice being inscrutable," said Susanna. "Men are fascinated by female mystery."

"Practice being friendly," said Honey. "Men like friendly gals. Ask Bill over for a piece of pie."

On Sunday nights of the school year they listened to the radio. The Manhattan Merry-go-Round, Phil Spitalny and his All Girl Orchestra, Charlie McCarthy, Jack Benny and Eddie Cantor, until the staccato notes of the Richfield Reporter signaled their bedtime.

They checked Best Sellers out of the public library — *Anthony Adverse, How Green Was My*

Valley, Rebecca, Gone with the Wind, All This, and Heaven Too — fat cream-colored volumes printed on tissue thin pages, smelling divinely of ink.

They went to movies. They saw Sophisticated Comedies, mostly. Ginger Rogers in feathers, like an exotic bird, floating down the marble staircase of a Luxury Hotel. Fred Astaire — dapper, urbane — dancing "Cheek to Cheek." Cary Grant or Ray Milland or William Powell mixing martinis in a chic white-carpeted penthouse, while Carole Lombard or Constance Bennett or Katie Hepburn sat on a white divan, fondling a dirty, orphaned mongrel dog.

Love — witty, irreverent, lighthearted — conquered All. It conquered Mistaken Identity, False Rumors of Death, Divorce, the Curse of a Noble Title, or a Great Fortune, Genial Crooks, Pixilated Old Ladies and Sordid Politics.

"I am madly madly in love with Cary Grant," said Janet insincerely. "When he walked into that bedroom, I could have died."

They saw sad movies, too. Honey, in those days, had a natural predilection for sorrow.

"*Dark Victory,* she goes blind, you know, and then there's that other one, he just walks into the sea."

"Where is Honey, she's always late?" said Janet.

"Put your purse on that seat and save it for her. She's going to miss *The March of Time*. My father says Hitler has done a lot for Germany, only he's going a bit too far."

"Here she comes."

"Late as usual."

"Honey, here! We saved your seat."

"Sssh, that man is looking at us."

"You missed *The March of Time!*"

After the movie they emerged into daylight with blinking eyes. The sunlit world seemed unreal. Pleasantly dazed, they walked to the Cozy Nook for rainbow Cokes.

"My face is all puffy from crying," said Honey, examining herself in a pocket mirror. "I look like a pig."

"Will they serve pigs at the Cozy Nook?" said Susanna.

"There is no rule against it," Janet said.

Susanna, who tended toward fantasy, and, who later fought this tendency by the study of facts, went on — "and, well, someone walks by, who knows us, you know, and nods, and then, seeing this pig, just sitting there, takes a second look, like what's his name does in the *Pete Smith Specialties*, and —"

"And he or she?" said Janet.

"She," said Susanna. "She goes home and calls

one of our mothers and says, 'Did you know your daughter hangs around with pigs?' "

"I know who it was who did that," said Janet.

"Who?" said Honey. The puffiness in her face had subsided; she had helped it by smoothing out her skin with the tips of her fingers.

"Evajean Treece."

"Evajean wouldn't do a thing like that," said Honey. "In the first place, she wouldn't dare."

"She calls anonymously. She puts a handkerchief over the mouthpiece."

"But for heaven's sakes, why?"

"She wants to destroy the Trio."

A chill fell over the group at Janet's words.

Then Honey began to giggle. "Well, that settles her," she said. "She's beginning to be a bore, anyhow. She called me three times last night while I was trying to put up my hair."

"Try reading the classics," Janet said. "Read a classic once a month. It will improve your mind. By the way, I found out how to get an abortion, yesterday."

"How did you find out?"

"I read this article. You go to Mexico."

"Well, how do you go to Mexico, for heaven's sakes," said Honey. "I can just see my parents, if I tell them I'm going to Mexico."

"You go on the Greyhound," said Susanna.

"And you're met by a man in a mask, and you have your abortion and he never takes off his mask."

"Well, I can just see my mother if I just said I was going to Mexico."

"You say you have to go to an International Conference of the Campfire Girls," Susanna said.

"She might think that was better than hanging around with pigs."

"But I *am* the pig. You forgot."

"Can't you just see this pig going to Mexico to have an abortion?" said Susanna. "I mean, imagine — !"

"Everyone is being much too silly. People are looking at us. We must have more dignity," said Janet.

"I simply have to have another Coke," Honey said.

"Cokes are full of calories, and cause pimples," said Susanna.

"I don't care, I'm going to die if I don't have one, it's all been too much!"

One spring afternoon, when the girls were sunbathing around the McKittrick pool, doing their nails and listening to Artie Shaw's "Frenesi" on Honey's portable radio, Bennet Tidewater, who was a year older than they, and a senior in high

school, and whom they knew to be strange, looked
over the backyard fence and said, "I shall be serv-
ing tea in half an hour if you would care to come."

The girls were dumbstruck at such a formal,
quaint invitation; then they began to giggle.

"Please be prompt and stop giggling," Bennet
said, and disappeared.

Smothering their giggles, they went into the Mc-
Kittrick house and washed their hands and feet
and dressed and combed their hair, and then they
walked to Bennet's house in a straight file like
proper young ladies from a convent. It was a false
act of self-discipline; they were prepared to ex-
plode with laughter, afterwards.

Susanna rang the bell. Bennet, wearing old tan
pants and an old brown sweater with a clean white
shirt underneath it, answered the door. They saw
from his expression he would brook no nonsense.

"Please come in," said Bennet, and led the way.

They followed him into the dark house, which
was immaculate, but had an impoverished air.
There was an old varnished German upright
piano, a heavy worn sofa and a matching armchair,
with lace antimacassars on their thick arms. As
they climbed the stairs, they saw framed photographs of Bennet on the wall; at the landing was
Bennet's junior high school diploma.

Susanna remembered that Mrs. Tidewater, a

quiet, soft-spoken small woman, played the piano at Miss Ivy's dance studio. In the daytime she took occasional piano students. Susanna, curled up quietly in a chair in the McKittrick living room, had once heard Mrs. McKittrick complain to the Doctor that the piano students lowered the tone of the neighborhood.

"What's she supposed to do, starve?" Dr. McKittrick had said. "Her husband was an alcoholic who left them years ago."

As if Bennett were reading Susanna's thoughts, now, he said, "My mother refuses to let me work. To make up for this, I do all the housekeeping and cooking. This way, please."

Susanna felt a kinship toward Bennet; they both were in charge of households.

Bennet led them down a shabby hall to his room. He opened the door, and the three girls gasped in wonder. It was like a luxurious cave from the *Arabian Nights.*

The floor was covered with an old Oriental rug; his bed was covered with an East Indian bedspread. There were brightly colored cushions with tassels on the floor; in one corner of the room stood a chipped white plaster Corinthian pillar.

"From the old Brink house. I salvaged it when it was torn down," Bennet said.

There was a Victorian cherry bureau, and, on

the bureau stood a baroque silver tea set, highly polished. Water was boiling in a kettle on a hot plate on the floor. On the wall was a watercolor, signed by Bennett, of the Tidewater coat of arms. Over his bed hung a wooden crucifix he had carved himself.

"Sit down, please."

The girls sat down on the cushions.

Bennet made the tea, not from tea bags, but elaborately, in the proper manner, and served it to them in chipped, eggshell-thin, white cups. Then he sat down among them and said, "What are your goals in life?"

Janet, who was usually the boldest, said, "I should like to improve my character."

"What are you doing toward this end?" said Bennet.

Janet blushed.

"You must practice self-control and learn not to blush," said Bennet, severely. He turned to Susanna. "Next," he said.

"I should like to learn all there is to know, and then write about it," Susanna said.

"That is greedy," said Bennet, "not to mention impossible. That was the sin of Faust."

"Faust?" said Susanna.

"He was a man who sold his soul in order to discover the secrets of the Universe."

"Oh, I didn't have anything in mind like that," Susanna said. "I mean — more —"

"Gossip?" said Bennet.

"Well, more about people," Susanna said.

"How are your powers of observation?" Bennet said. He put a hand over his eyes and said, "What color are my eyes?"

Susanna thought, and said, "Brown."

"Green, flecked with brown," Bennet said. He looked at Honey. "What about you?" he said.

"I want to be a scientist and find a cure for leprosy," said Honey. Bennet gave her a piercing look, but asked her no questions.

When they had finished their tea, Bennet put a Mozart quartet on his phonograph. He explained that he only cared for eighteenth century music, at the moment. Then the conversation became more animated.

"I've taken all the tests in the magazines," Janet said. "When I look up my score, it always says, 'You need to find a way for more self-expression,' or 'You must make more of an effort to realize your potential.'"

"No one knows what makes a person the way he is," said Bennet. "It is one of the mysteries of existence — take me, for instance. I want to do something big before I die. That's very important to me. The only really big thing I can think of is to risk my life for some good cause. Perhaps I shall offer myself for cancer research or carry Christianity into the jungles of New Guinea. Following that, if I survive, I shall marry. Not for love. I want to strengthen the Tidewater chin." He pointed to his own chin. "It's getting weaker every generation. I'm going to marry a girl with a strong chin. A *mariage de convenance.* I shall do my best to make my wife happy, of course. I hope that love will grow out of our mutual efforts for self-sacrifice. I believe strongly in the sanctity of the home."

The girls stayed for two hours. Afterwards, they retired to Honey's room.

"Well, that was spooky," said Janet. But she did not sound convinced.

"I guess he's a pansy," Honey said. But her voice was oddly subdued.

" 'I only care for eighteenth century music at the moment,' " mimicked Susanna. Then she added, "I suppose there's a lot we can learn from him, though."

During the next year they drank tea in Bennet's room many times.

Slowly, silently, now the moon
Walks the night in her silver shoon;
This way, and that, she peers, and sees
Silver fruit upon silver trees —

read Miss Louise Henderson, one of Norton High's English teachers, in her poetry voice to the Trio whom she had invited for an Evening. Miss Henderson's Evenings coincided with the adult Red Cross life saving lessons at the Natatorium where her roommate, Miss Maribell Turknet, Norton High's girls gym and hygiene teacher, taught.

Capturing the Trio for her very own was a feat, and Miss Henderson did not propose sharing them with Miss Turknet. Miss Turknet was large, square-shouldered and husky-voiced, and she bullied pretty, fading Miss Henderson and tried to run her life. The Trio was aware of this; Miss Henderson had confided in them; they were "for" Miss Henderson, but, at the same time, they enjoyed the rivalry their presence inspired.

"Turky does not care for poetry," said Miss Henderson, now, in her After-School Voice. "Of course," she added, "that is her loss. She threw a dreadful scene last night, and I'm sure the neighbors heard and we will be tossed out, and lose our jobs to boot."

"What happened?" said Susanna.

"I was making the cookies for this evening. Minding my own business, just making cookies, when Turky said, 'How long is this mess in the kitchen going to last?' It was jealousy, pure jealousy, her classes loathe her, all she does is blow that dreadful whistle and shout commands, but I thought I would suddenly burst. I said, 'I intend to clean up after I finish. At least I don't smoke, and leave ashes around,' and she turned to me and said, and I swear these were her very words, she said, 'Smoking is my own business. I indulge in it after work, but I don't bring my classes into our home.' Can you imagine? I don't bring my classes into our home! Who would want to come if she asked them? And what would they talk about? The Systems of the Body? Her life is so empty, so devoid of anything beautiful and fine, I don't see how she can stand it. I pity her."

"Why don't you live by yourself?" said Honey.

Miss Henderson smiled wanly. "I thought you

might ask that. Indeed, why don't I? Because she needs me, poor thing. I can't just abandon her. I would be afraid of what she might do. She's a very violent woman, actually. Well, now, at least you know why the cookies aren't better. I think I forgot part of the sugar, I was so shaken."

"They're divine," murmured the Trio, munching.

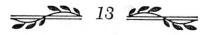

13

THERE WERE ALSO BOYS. There was Vince Holbrook and Buzzy Heffelfinger, and Nathan Brenner and Teddy Lyons, and from time to time, miscellaneous others. They congregated at the McKittrick house, not entirely because Honey was the prettiest of the three, but because the household made them so welcome — Mrs. McKittrick with her lavish hospitality, and Dr. McKittrick with his easy manners and merry spirit. It might also be said that the older McKittricks served another useful purpose; they acted as a kind of buffer between the boys and the Trio; the boys could tell themselves they were calling upon the entire family, rather than its nubile member.

On a springtime Saturday evening, Buzzy's ancient 1927 Model T would circle the block. Oouuga, its horn would go. It was both ceremonial trumpet and comic relief. It heralded springtime, love and mystery. The Trio, gathered at the McKittrick house, would wait, restlessly; Mrs. McKittrick would take off her apron and pat her hair; even Dr. McKittrick would feel the tension and find it difficult to concentrate on the *News Sentinel.*

Then there would be a crunch of gravel in the driveway, and the oouuga would sound outside the door.

At this point, Dr. McKittrick would make his speech. "No daughter of mine answers a horn," he would say. "You will have to wait until they ring the doorbell."

But, at last, the doorbell would ring, and the Trio, overwhelmed at their victory, would rush upstairs to Honey's room. Mrs. McKittrick would answer the door.

"Why, hello there," she would cry, and her surprise was so convincing she believed it herself. "Why, hello there, come on in."

Then she would go to the bottom of the stairs

and call the girls; this duty performed, she seemed to forget she was not the heroine of the drama. Her cheeks would grow flushed, her eyes, starry; she would lead the boys into the living room.

"Now, I want to show you something, but you must promise to be honest," she would say. "My family is no help at all. Do you think this is too much red?"

"Oh, for God's sakes, you're not boring them with those damn samples, are you?" Dr. McKittrick would say. "Now, look here, gentlemen, don't betray me. I like that sofa the way it is, it's the only comfortable piece of furniture in the whole damn house."

"They don't mind, they want to help me!" she cried, and the young men, seduced by her aggressive charms, would smile and nod uneasily. They did not like betraying their own sex, but they sensed that Dr. McKittrick wanted them to please her.

At Christmas time she showed them the Tree. "It isn't right at all. It's too stubby, here, and too thin in here. Honey and the Doctor just throw the tinsel on. I'm going to have to take every piece off and put it back. Don't you agree?"

"Say one word against that tree, and I'll toss you all out," the Doctor would say. "It's a fine tree, it looks just fine the way it is. Every Christmas we go through this. It's a dandy tree, isn't it, Vince? We ain't gonna get another!"

When the Trio came downstairs, the boys would already be at home; it was almost as if the girls were an intrusion.

"Oh, Mother, really," Honey might say, but mildly, for she, too, at this particular time in her life, found her mother's machinations a protection.

Mrs. McKittrick would then disappear into the kitchen, and emerge with one of her productions — platters of small elegant sandwiches, or trays of cheeses and ham and salami, embellished with olives and pickles and curlicues of radish and celery. It looked like a colored photograph from *House and Garden,* and awed the boys into an uneasy silence. "It is pretty, if I do say so myself," she would say.

"It is pretty if I do say so myself," Janet Kroner, née Springer, would say in later years when she became a decorator, standing back a bit to admire something she had assembled. But her tone of voice was lighter; there was a note of sophisticated depreciation, which provided a leeway in case her client did not agree. She was never able to achieve Mrs. McKittrick's childlike egotism, which was also the egotism of the artist or the insane.

After this, Dr. McKittrick would break the ice. "So that's where my favorite rat cheese has been," he would say. "You hide it from me, and now you're going to waste it on company. Try a piece of rat cheese, boys, you may as well appreciate something good."

One terrible night, weevils were discovered, swarming all over an especially elaborate plate of hors d'oeuvres, and everyone became hysterical, laughing at Mrs. McKittrick's horror.

"It's because you keep buying new boxes of crackers, and never use up the old ones," the Doctor said. "Why, I bet you have a dozen boxes of open crackers in that cupboard."

"It's the heat. I'm going to call the exterminator the first thing in the morning," Mrs. McKittrick cried.

"We don't mind a few thousand weevils, do we, boys?"

"Oh, Daddy," said Honey.

"Make him stop, please," begged Mrs. McKittrick, who was close to tears. "I've never been so humiliated in all my life."

"Oh, Mother!" Honey said.

Mrs. McKittrick flounced out of the room, and up the stairs. They could hear her bedroom door slam.

There was an uneasy silence. Then the Doctor said, "Pass the weevils around, boys, while I go up and apologize to my wife."

On most nights, after the opening ceremonies, the Doctor would leave the living room first. He would go into a smaller room, off the living room, which Mrs. McKittrick called the den, and had decorated with a hunting motif — lamps made from duck decoys, and bird prints on the walls, and an old shotgun she had bought in a second-hand store over the fireplace.

"All we need is a few stuffed deers' heads," the Doctor used to say. "Isn't it a pity I don't hunt?"

He would listen to the ten o'clock Richfield Reporter, and then return for Mrs. McKittrick.

"Well, it's time I got my beauty sleep," he would say. "See you in the spring."

Mrs. McKittrick would join him ruefully.

Then records were put on the phonograph, and lights were dimmed, and the young people would dance.

On hot nights they would swim or play children's games — Sardine, Kick the Can, or Beckon Beckon. Occasionally, younger children in the neighborhood would join them. They would lie huddled together in the warm darkness, under a porch, or on the cellar steps, the physical intimacy of these occasions charging the air with excitement. There was a sense of unrealized possibilities, of a future, sweet and amorphous, like a fairy tale.

Usually the Trio would spend the night together in Honey's room, afterwards, talking far into the morning.

"I am madly in love with Teddy Lyons," said Honey, insincerely.

"Did you notice how Vince attached himself to Janet?" said Susanna.

"Vince likes Honey, I happen to know," said Janet, who, being tall and awkward (though possessing good bones), found it hard to believe anyone could prefer her.

"Teddy is a dear, I adore his little limp, it's a congenital defect," Honey said.

"Vince is just trying to make Honey jealous," said Janet. "He knows she likes Buzzy best."

"Do I?" said Honey, dreamily. "Well, of course, I do like Buzzy. But, tonight, I sort of noticed Teddy, for the first time."

"It's you and Buzzy in the yearbook this year. They have you down as a couple," Janet said.

Honey giggled. "Well, if the yearbook says so — And I do like him."

"Nathan is very shy, he's intellectual, but you can tell he's partial to Susanna," said Janet.

"It's just because we're both leftovers," said Susanna cheerfully.

"You mustn't think of yourself that way," said Janet, who was fighting this tendency in herself.

"How must I think of myself?"

"You are a Queen —"

"And everyone else is my subject," Susanna said, with a grin.

"I like Nathan, too. I adore shy boys," said Honey. "But tonight, when I was hiding under the porch with Buzzy —"

"Yes?" said Janet.

"Yes?" said Susanna.

"Nothing, really. He just — became affectionate."

"What is your definition of affection?" said Janet.

"I don't really have one, I guess. He pressed my hand, and —"

"And?" said Janet and Susanna.

Honey sighed, heavily. "I don't know, it's hard to explain, he sort of kissed me, I suppose."

"You suppose?" said Janet. "How can you just suppose a thing like that?"

"Now that I think about it, I'm not terribly sure it happened."

"Oh, Honey!" both girls groaned.

Honey giggled. "Well, I couldn't testify in court that it did," she said.

"The yearbook was right," said Janet.

"I'm not sure, there is Teddy —"

"Oh, Honey!" said Janet, in a disgusted tone.

But, at this time, their allegiance to the Trio was stronger than their allegiance to any single boy.

When it was necessary to pair off for a date occasionally, they did it this way. Vince, who was sober and kind and responsible, took Janet, and Nathan, who was quiet and intellectual and withdrawn, took Susanna, and Buzzy, who was sappy and humorous and high-spirited and popular, took Honey.

But these arrangements had a kind of fluid quality; there was no attempt to solidify them. For the boys were in love with the Trio more than any of its single parts.

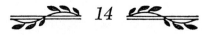 14

BENNET TIDEWATER said, "Something is bound to happen."

"What sort of a something?" said Susanna.

"We must wait and see."

The something that happened happened to Honey, and, in this way, of course, happened to the Trio, too. It happened in the spring of 1941, when the Trio were in their senior year in high school. What happened was that Honey, always the prettiest of the Trio, became beautiful.

It was more of a shock to Honey than to anyone else. She was not at all certain how to respond to it. She began to study herself carefully in mirrors, in the black marble surface of the Farmers and Merchants Bank, in the shiny stainless steel of paper napkin holders, in the polished surface of new cars — in any object that would hold her reflection — and, there it was, there was no getting away from it; it was a fact of life, like having a disease.

She looked like debutante Brenda Diana Duff Frazier. She had long dark hair, parted in the center, and blue blue eyes, and milky skin, just like the Skin You Love to Touch. Something had happened underneath her clothes, too. When she undressed at night, she examined this occurrence in the full-length mirror on the back of her closet door, which had been put there to check her stocking seams and hems. There were firm little breasts that over the months swelled like ripe Norton pears. Her hips grew rounder; her waist smaller. Her bottom, when she turned around, was especially pleasing; it was rosy and heart-shaped, like a Valentine.

"Beauty is as Beauty does," said Mrs. McKittrick, noticing her daughter staring into the antique gold mirror over the fireplace, one day.

Honey knew this was a lie. Beauty is not as beauty does; beauty just is. She had not been aware, before, that her mother was capable of lying to her. People only lied when they were scared. Beauty was evidently something that scared them; it was a kind of threat. She felt both hurt and guilty — hurt at the frailness of her mother's moral nature; guilty that she was the cause of its disintegration.

Was this something she could discuss with the Trio? She decided it was not. For the first time in her life, she felt alone.

=≥≥≥— 15 —≤≤≤

ONE MAY AFTERNOON, Mrs. McKittrick was in the garden, dressed, as she later told her husband, in "my horrible garden dress with no stockings on," when Elaine, their present "girl," told her that Father Gerhardt, the Episcopal minister, was in the living room.

"I was absolutely horrified," Mrs. McKittrick said. "I don't see what right ministers have to just drop in on you like that without any notice. In the first place, I'm not even an Episcopalian, I'm a Congregationalist, and there isn't even any Congregationalist church in town. I said to myself, what is he after? I haven't been to church, except when Honey was confirmed, but I don't even belong to his old church. And we support it, don't we? I thought, he's after money, they're always after money, something is always going wrong, the parish roof is leaking or the furnace has gone out. But if he wanted money, why didn't he go to you? Oh, I was trembling with annoyance, I can assure you! I rushed to the kitchen door and up the back stairs, on tiptoe, so he wouldn't hear, and I pulled on a pair of stockings and combed my hair, that's all I had time for, and then I went down. Dressed, if you can imagine, in my old garden clothes!"

"Well?" said Dr. McKittrick. "What did he have to say?"

"What did he have to say? What didn't he have to say would be a better question! You can't imagine, it's beyond belief."

"Tell it in chronological order," Dr. McKittrick suggested.

"Well, that's what I am doing. He said, it's a hot day, isn't it? I should think, the way they dress, in those high collars, he would have been expired, I was drenched clear through, myself, but, after all, I hadn't counted on a visitor. So I said, yes, it certainly is, would you care for lemonade or a glass of sherry, and he took sherry — Episcopals can — and then he said, what a lovely home, he is a nice man, you know, he was terribly kind to the Marshes when their daughter eloped with that Jewish man, he told them, Christ was a Jew, they had never thought of that, and —"

"What did he have to say to you?" said the Doctor.

"I'm getting to that. He said, what a lovely home, and I said, thank you, only I was terrified he was about to ask me to open it up for the Ladies'

Rummage Sale, or some such thing, and then he admired my antiques, I must say he was discerning, he seemed to know old things, as few people do —"

"Is that why he came?"

"What do you mean, is that why he came?"

"To admire our home?"

"I only wish to God it were! We sat down, and drank some sherry, and then he said, I wanted to see you — it's about Honey."

"Honey?" said Dr. McKittrick. There was a sharpness in his voice.

"That's what he said, Honey, and my heart just sank. His face was very serious, and I thought, oh, my God, what has she done, and I said, Honey? And he said — do you know what he said then?"

"What did he say?"

"He said, she comes to church too much. Those were his words. She comes to church too much, he said. I just looked at him. I thought, aren't you supposed to go to church, for heaven's sakes? But I was wrong, all wrong. It seems it's a sin. The Catholics have a word for it, he said. I wrote it down so I'd remember. Here it is, it's called 'scrupulosity.'"

"Rubbish," said Dr. McKittrick.

"Yes. 'Scrupulosity.' That's what he called it. It means when you are using God for your own, I forget . . . well, personal reasons."

"Sounds pretty fancy-pants to me."

"You see, she doesn't just go to church on Sundays, she goes every morning to eight o'clock communion. I didn't even know there was eight o'clock communion. She goes before school. Father Gerhardt says it's mostly for old ladies."

"Well, as long as it's old ladies, we better worry," Dr. McKittrick said.

"It isn't funny. There is more. He says she doesn't even approach the altar for communion, sometimes, as if she had decided she wasn't worthy of — drinking His blood and eating His body — those were his words. I was brought up Congregationalist, and frankly, it all seems unhealthy to me. But she just kneels and prays, while others go up. He thinks she has some problem. Can you imagine?"

"Of course I can imagine. Why shouldn't she have problems? Who doesn't?"

"But, at her age —"

"Precisely at her age."

"And so pretty and healthy. I could picture Susanna, or even Janet, they've both been brought up so oddly. But not Honey."

"Honey has a right to problems, too."

"Well, anyway, I said I would see what I could find out, and I was so grateful he came to see me, though he certainly might have called, first —"

"Did you say that?"

"What?"

"That he might have called first?"

"Of course I didn't say that. He said, if there was anything he could do, if Honey would care to talk to him, please let him know, and I said I would ask her, and then he asked me if that was a New England chest, the maple one in the hall, he is from New England, you know, and his grandmother had a chest like that."

"Have you said anything to Honey yet?"

"Well, of course I did. I said, Father Gerhardt paid a nice little visit and he says you're in church too much, he says it's a sin called 'scrupulosity,' and she said, why doesn't that old fogey mind his own business, but not to worry because she was never going near his old church again, and I said, he was just trying to help, that is his job, and she said, well, tell him not to try to help me, and she stormed upstairs, and slammed the door to her room. I followed her up. I said, Honey, I am your mother, and I want to help, and she screamed back, she didn't need any help, thank you. I feel all sick inside. Do you suppose she's in some sort of trouble?"

"We must wait and see."

"It is obvious you aren't a mother."

"It would be obvious, in any case."

"I've thought about talking to Janet, perhaps she can help."

"Oh, for Pete's sakes, don't talk to Janet. That would be all wrong, Janet is part of the Trio."

"Well, that's just it. Janet will be concerned because she *is* part of the Trio."

"You must not talk to Janet," Dr. McKittrick said.

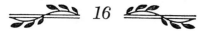 *16*

"I've been hoping to catch you alone," said Mrs. McKittrick to Janet a few days later. "I want to talk to you. It's about Honey. I'm awfully worried. Shall we sit down? Just toss those wallpaper samples on the table, there. I've been meaning to ask your opinion about them. I'm doing the downstairs bathroom over, but I'm too upset to think clearly. I was thinking of luggage tan."

They sat down together on Mrs. McKittrick's red sofa.

"Luggage tan with brown towels, with luggage tan monograms," Mrs. McKittrick said.

"That should be lovely," said Janet. "You have such scrumptious taste."

"Well, of course, it's just a hobby. I have had people tell me I ought to turn professional, but I couldn't do that."

"You could," said Janet. "You honestly could."

"It's nice to be appreciated. My own family doesn't care about such things. For all it matters to them, they could live in a barn."

"You were saying — about Honey?"

"Oh, yes. Have you noticed anything different — or strange?"

"Now that you mention it, there have been *things*. What have you noticed?"

"Father Gerhardt was here. I shall never feel the same about that man, again, even if he did admire my antiques. He came with no warning at all. I barely had time to pull my stockings on."

"What did he say?"

"It has a technical name. I don't like to burden you, dear."

"You mustn't worry about me."

"It's called 'scrupulosity.' "

"I see."

"It means she goes to morning communion every day before school."

So that's where she's been, thought Janet. "I see," she said, again.

"It's a sin, you know, to go to church too much."

"It's an emotional thing," said Janet. "Sex, obviously."

"Sex?" said Mrs. McKittrick. "You really think so?"

Janet nodded.

"I was thinking that, myself. But I'm not sure I quite know what you mean, exactly, by sex. You girls are all so modern nowadays. In my time, we didn't dare use such a word. You don't mean anything bad by it, do you?"

"It depends, of course, on what you mean by 'bad.'"

"You know, I can't say it, but you must understand a mother's feelings, it isn't easy being a mother, but I do my best."

"I suppose you mean is Honey still a virgin?" said Janet. Though she managed to keep her voice cool, her question was a tremendous experiment.

Mrs. McKittrick looked startled, then she beamed. "Yes, of course, that's what I mean. You modern girls are so clever. That's what I mean, precisely. You couldn't have said it better. You have cheered me immensely."

"But I haven't answered your question."

"What question was that?"

"You wanted to know if — that is — is — Honey?"

"So I did." Mrs. McKittrick giggled.

Janet's experiment had succeeded beyond her wildest hopes. She was, in fact, shocked by Mrs. McKittrick's giggle; she did not consider it seemly.

"My mother was from New England," Mrs. McKittrick said. "She brought me up like a Victorian. But I'm not a prude. I try to look at things in the modern way, you know. Don't you think I do?"

"You have a very youthful outlook," said Janet, who was now beginning to be bored. "As far as I know, I'm sure she is."

"Oh, I've never doubted it for a moment," Mrs. McKittrick said. "It reminds me of my courtship days. You won't believe it, but when I got married, I didn't really know what went on. I'm sure Honey doesn't, either. I've always told the Doctor, you should tell me things, I won't be shocked, but you know how men are. Doctors, especially. Your generation is so much luckier."

"The Trio has taken a solemn oath to tell all to one another," said Janet, taking this opportunity to return to the subject. "But I think Honey is betraying this oath."

"It makes me very sad. We've always been like sisters. She told me everything, too. Oh, I don't mean Trio secrets, of course. And now, this terrible blow. Going to church every day, without my knowing."

It occurred to Janet that Honey had substituted God for the Trio; it was the first time, but not the last, that she was jealous of Honey and God.

"You must let me know if anything special happens," Janet said.

"Oh, I will, of course. It's such a comfort talking to you. You've always seemed so much more mature than the rest of the Trio. I've always remarked on that to the Doctor."

"What does he say?"

"Oh, you know how men are. He's such a dear, but he doesn't understand this sort of thing. He thinks all of you are still children."

"Men are that way." Janet sighed, solemnly. "We must put up with it."

"Of course, you mustn't breathe a word to Honey about our little chat."

"Cross my heart."

"I'd like to show you the samples, if you don't mind. I've always felt you had a feeling for color. My family is no help at all. You really think luggage tan is all right for a bathroom? I considered avocado green."

"Let's take a look," said Janet.

In the bathroom, Mrs. McKittrick held up the wallpaper sample. "There, what do you think? Please be honest."

Janet took three small steps backwards, and

peered at the wall through narrowed eyes. "Luggage tan, absolutely," she said.

She knew her treachery was now complete.

 *17*

PEOPLE, INCLUDING JANET AND SUSANNA, treated Honey differently, now. Though often it was in very subtle ways, she sensed it, and it made her feel more lonely. It was as if, she thought, she had turned overnight into a witch.

Well, if she were a witch, that was that, she decided, out of desperation. She would use her new power; they had left her no choice. All her energies and talents would have to go into learning how to manipulate it. She could no longer find a refuge in church. Scrupulosity must give way to a lack of scruples. She could no longer help the lepers or worry over grades or read the classics or make a pet of a poor girl or read self-help articles in magazines. She must leave all these things in back of her and devote herself to her new calling.

In order to work this all out more clearly in her mind, she paid a visit to Bennet one Thursday afternoon.

Bennet had graduated from high school, but he had decided he could not go to college and leave his mother alone. Moreover, he had come to the conclusion that he could do as well or better, using the public library in Norton.

"Independent studies," he had told the Trio, with a laugh. He had added that later he intended to study abroad.

Now he sold sheet music at the Melody Shop and played the organ at St. Matthew's Episcopal on Sundays and for choir practice. Thursday was his only day off.

"I can no longer help the lepers," Honey told him, as they sat in his room.

Bennet nodded, wisely.

"What should I do?"

"No one can tell you. Of course, you are not the first this has happened to. There was Helen and Cleopatra and Héloïse and Francesca — All of them caused a great deal of trouble, poor things."

"I don't want to cause trouble," Honey said.

"It is a great responsibility," said Bennet. "In the old days, girls could be sent to convents. You are running around loose. I think, probably, you ought to marry early, as soon as possible. Have children. I would consider you myself, if you had a stronger chin."

"There are Buzzy and Vince and Teddy," Honey said. But, even as she said their names, she knew they were not right.

"They will all make good husbands, eventually," said Bennet. "But I think perhaps you ought to marry an older man — someone who will appreciate your loveliness, who will understand its rarity and its importance. Someone who, for some reason, is aware of the transitory nature of such things. 'When old age shall this generation waste, Thou shalt remain' — but that, unfortunately, was written about a vase."

Honey sighed, heavily.

"It can't be helped. It would be much easier for you if you weren't beautiful. It will be harder on you than others, when physical decay sets in."

"That will be some time from now, won't it?"

"Yes, but it will still come as a surprise. Your whole life will be centered around being beautiful — all your little ways, so charming now, will suddenly have no meaning. I can say all this because you're not really listening."

"Sorry."

"For example, the manner in which you toss your head, so that a lock of hair falls over one eye. How will that look on an aged, wrinkled woman? You should take steps to prepare yourself, now."

"What sort of steps?"

"There is only one sort of step and that is spiritual."

"I shall never set foot in that filthy church, again. Except maybe for my wedding."

"Father Gerhardt was only trying to help. Unfortunately, he is human, as I have discovered myself. He should have gone to you, and not to your mother. Well, perhaps, in the meantime, you should enjoy your blessings. What was your confirmation text?"

" 'Stir up the gift.' "

"That should do nicely, for a time. By the way, beware of Janet Springer."

"Of Janet? For heaven's sakes, why?"

"She will be your enemy."

"But what could Janet do? We're Best Friends! We're part of the Trio."

"You lack a tragic sense of life," said Bennet. "That's because you don't believe in the existence of Evil. You can't help it, it's the way you've been brought up. But I find it very frightening, myself."

"Oh, dear, I seem to frighten everyone. You make me sound like some sort of monster."

"You are, in a way. All three of you girls are monsters in that you are amoral. I suspect, in the long run, you are the most monstrous because you have more power to hurt people. Would you care for some tea?"

"Doesn't tea do something bad to your complexion?"

"My tea is a special brand and contains no impurities," Bennet said.

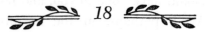 *18*

IT WAS ANOTHER THURSDAY. Susanna said, "Once I stood up on our roof at night, and I could look into Dr. and Mrs. McKittrick's bedroom, the blinds were open, and guess what I saw?"

"I am not going to guess," said Bennet. "You give me the shudders."

"I saw Dr. McKittrick naked, dancing a sailor's hornpipe, while Mrs. McKittrick clapped her hands."

Bennet said nothing, but looked extremely severe.

"Do you want to know how many people I've seen naked, not counting kids?"

"I do not."

"I don't see why," said Susanna. "You're the only one who knows, and you won't tell. And I don't do it for bad reasons, not very bad, anyhow. I do it because I have this awful curiosity."

"I can see you want to talk about yourself. Very well, what sort of person do you think you are?"

"Proud. I have this terrible pride. And sneaky. I've been brought up strangely. The fact is, I've brought myself up. I suppose I've always envied Honey for having a real family."

"Real families can be a problem, too. How long do you intend to subjugate your individuality to this mystical body?"

"What mystical body?"

"I'm speaking, naturally, of the Trio."

"What else is there for me to do?"

"I assume you are asking a genuine question." He looked at her closely. She still possessed her urchin scrawniness; there seemed to be no sign of breasts or hips. Her straw-colored hair fell limply about her thin face. Only her features had grown larger.

"At your age, many young ladies assume an interest in the opposite sex."

"The opposite sex has to be interested in you, too."

"Perhaps you're not exactly in the current style. But that might be remedied."

"How?"

"Well, your hair, for example —"

"It's horrid."

"Not at all. It just isn't fashionable. The opposite

sex are usually too conventional or too frightened to look beyond the prevailing mode. I can fix your hair for you."

Before she knew what he was doing, he had led her into his bathroom, and had doused her head in the basin. He shampooed it meticulously, with deft, positive movements; then he brushed it until it was partly dry. After this, he fetched his mother's curlers, and set her hair into a pageboy.

Then he stepped back and looked at her. "You could use some color in your lips," he said. He went out of the room again and came back with a Tangee lipstick, and applied it, deftly, to her mouth. While her hair was drying, he read to her from *Wine from These Grapes* by Edna St. Vincent Millay.

Susanna did not care much for the contents, but the deep, pleasant sound of his voice was reassuring.

After a time, he put the book down, and said, "*Now.*"

He took out the curlers and brushed her hair, vigorously, then combed it. Then he stepped back to admire his work; suddenly, he doubled over. Susanna thought he had a pain, but it was laughter. With a tremendous effort — he was laughing so hard — he managed to hand her the silver-backed mirror from his dressing table set. At first, when she looked, the shock paralyzed her. Then she got into the spirit, too. Together they rolled about on the floor, shrieking hysterically.

Bennet, who was so good with his hands, ordinarily, had made her look, they decided, exactly like Arthur, the McKittricks' spaniel.

Still howling with laughter, Susanna stumbled into the bathroom and doused her head in the basin to get out the "Arthur" set.

After that, they sat cross-legged on pillows on the floor, and Bennet poured tea. "I think we might consider that experiment a failure," he said, slowly. "Shall we direct our attention to other things?"

Susanna said, "I am ready."

"Very well. You say you want to be a writer. This is a new breakfast tea. Compare it, please, with the old tea."

She took a studied sip. "It's bitterer."

"Not bitter, precisely. Find the exact word."

"Stronger, then?"

"Yes, stronger. It's hard to get you to concentrate properly. You're too involved with your own feelings. All of you Trio are. Now, involvement with one's own feelings gets in the way of honest, direct observation. You say you have this terrible curiosity. You like to watch people, and, indeed, there is a great deal to watch. But, if you are going to be a writer, you will have to train yourself to be a more accurate observer. Later, perhaps, you can branch off from there and get beyond mere facts, though I am not at all certain you have that sort of largeness of spirit. But, for the moment, stick with facts. Start with objects, instead of people. Objects are easier, though even they have a way of eluding you. Describe the Rialto Theatre."

"The Rialto Theatre, let's see," said Susanna. "Well, outside there's this big marquee, and arcade, and inside little balconies that lead nowhere. Sort of Arabian Nightsie."

"This won't do at all," Bennet said. "The Rialto Theatre is neo-Venetian Gothic with polychrome masonry patterning, showing Oriental and Moorish influences. You must learn to be more precise. You must learn to look. Your assignment for next time will be the Union Building at Fourth and Main, and St. Matthew's Episcopal."

"What has this to do with the Trio?" said Susanna.

"That's just it," Bennet said. "It has nothing to do with the Trio. Would you care for more tea?"

As they drank, they suddenly heard the piano downstairs. One of Mrs. Tidewater's pupils was struggling through Beethoven's Minuet in G.

 *19*

IT WAS ANOTHER THURSDAY. "Have you noticed anything different about Honey lately?" said Janet to Bennet.

"What sort of 'diff' "?

"It's hard to put your finger on, but she hardly seems part of the Trio anymore."

"Perhaps the Trio is failing her."

"Personally, I suspect it has to do with sex. Susanna saw her in a car with a college boy, but she has never mentioned it to either of us. Did she say anything to you?"

"It isn't easy being beautiful and popular," said Bennet, ignoring the question. "It's a great responsibility, in a way. There is a great deal she will have to give up. It's rather like being a nun, now that I think of it."

"Some nun. Have you seen her new gesture — the way she tosses her locks?"

"The Trio should exist to help its members, not to limit them," said Bennet. "Otherwise, it's a useless and decadent organization, which, like all other useless and decadent organizations, will collapse from its own inner rot."

"Without the Trio, I'm nothing," said Janet, bitterly.

"Hogwash," said Bennet. "You aren't being sincere."

"What do you mean?"

"It's the Trio that can't exist without you. You created it. Oh, of course, you had your reasons. It provides you with a milieu, a sense of importance. But if you want to keep it going, you have to be an individual, in your own right. Honey has all that taken care of for her at the moment, which is what scares you. Susanna is used to being independent — it's the way she has been brought up. If necessary, she could become a criminal. But, at the moment, you rely too much on the Trio. You must develop a sense of purpose of your own. This will not be easy."

"You can say that again," said Janet. "A sense of purpose is just what I don't have."

"Then we shall have to provide you with one. Marriage, I should think, eventually. Children. A happy home?" He spoke tentatively, as if he were testing these possibilities on Janet.

"I don't believe I'm the type people marry."

"Why not? If you had a stronger chin, I'd consider you, myself."

She smiled. "You don't understand, the thing is, I'm not sexually attractive."

Bennet put down his cup of tea, and gave her a long, studied look. "There's nothing really wrong," he said, after a moment. "You have an excellent bony structure."

"Nobody cares about bones, these days."

"The right person might."

"In Norton?" she asked, bitterly.

"Norton is not the world."

For the first time in her life, and with a sense of surprise, Janet considered this. She envisioned this world outside of Norton, rolling cinematically in a series of montages, like the beginning of the Pathé News or *The March of Time* — a world filled with soldiers and athletes and fashion models, a world where a good bony structure was as much appreciated as Honey's blooming contours. But it was still *another* world; a large black dot, which was Norton, remained fixed in a point outside of this cinematic vision. What a pity for her to have wasted her life on that dot!

"You are intelligent and more ambitious than either Honey or Susanna. I can see you leaving Norton. I would, myself, if it were not for my mother. But before you do, you must resolve things here, first, or they will always haunt you. Take the Trio, for example —"

The dot grew larger; the other, more dazzling world vanished, and with it, went Janet's courage. "Honey has destroyed the Trio," she said.

"If anyone destroys the Trio, it will be you. 'Each man kills the thing he loves.' Oscar Wilde wrote that in prison. You must try not to need the Trio so much, then it will thrive, and you will be free."

"You expect too much of people," she cried out in despair.

"Perhaps you expect too much of yourself. What do you think of this tea? I'm giving some to my mother for her birthday."

"Frankly, all tea tastes the same to me." With her courage gone, she could feel her pettiness increase. What was she doing here, listening to Bennet's moralizing? He had no close friends, himself; he could have no idea how she was suffering.

"Frankly, all tea tastes the same to me" was the closest Janet ever came to open rebellion with Bennet. But, after this, she no longer used him as a confidant.

"You expect too much of people," she told Dr. Kedy in later years.

"Perhaps you expect too much of yourself."

"That's funny, that's what Bennet Tidewater said."

20

ONE SATURDAY AFTERNOON Honey borrowed her mother's car to have her hair done at the Fountain of Beauty; Mrs. Mavis Gage, the beauty parlor operator, told Honey about a new facial treatment done with hot and cold towels which increased the circulation in the skin and made it glow. Honey had the facial. Afterwards, she drove to Janet's house to see if she noticed any difference.

No one was home but Mr. Springer. "It's so nice to see you, Honey, my dear," he said. He was wearing an old seersucker suit; Honey had never seen one before, except in an ad. He had a polka dot bow tie, and his hair was rather long. Honey thought he looked distinguished, like a Southern gentleman.

"I believe Janet and her mother have gone to do a bit of shopping. They should be back presently. Won't you come in and wait?"

Honey came in; she sat down on the old sofa in the barren, book-lined living room. Mr. Springer asked her if she would care for a glass of lemon-ade.

"I've been working on my History, and would enjoy a bit of a break. There's a pitcher in the refrigerator; Mrs. Springer makes it for me every day."

"That would be lovely, I guess," Honey said. She felt a bit awed by Mr. Springer's manners.

Mr. Springer brought the pitcher of lemonade and two glasses in upon a silver tray. There was also a bottle of gin on the tray.

"I often add a spot of gin, it helps my work," he said. "A Tom Collins. May I offer you one, too?"

"That would be lovely," said Honey, who had never had gin, but did not want to appear gauche before Mr. Springer.

Mr. Springer fixed the drinks, then presented one to Honey. He raised his glass. "Here's to Youth and Beauty," he said. He sat down on the sofa next to her. "I sometimes feel that Youth and Beauty is much absent from my life. But it is *within* me, nonetheless. And I can appreciate it when I see it. As, for instance, at this moment. I have not had the pleasure of seeing you for some time. You have grown into a most attractive young lady."

"Thank you, Mr. Springer," said Honey, primly. She sipped the lemonade, feeling a bit nervous.

Mr. Springer's presence was rather overpowering.

"Tell me something, child. Are you being courted by young men?"

Honey giggled. "Well, there are boys —" she said, awkwardly.

"Boys," said Mr. Springer, and sighed. He put his glass down, and laid one of his long, elegant hands upon Honey's knee. It seemed like a fatherly gesture. Yet she did not feel quite comfortable. "Boys around here are not exactly young gentlemen, wouldn't you say? I would imagine they might try to subject you to — ah — indignities. Has that ever happened, my dear?"

"Has — what — ever happened?" said Honey.

"Have you ever been approached indelicately?" said Mr. Springer.

Honey looked at him; his blue eyes had a curious glitter; his hand, upon her knee, had begun to tremble.

"Because, if they should," Mr. Springer went on, "and if you have no one to turn to, to give you advice, I should like you to know I would be most happy to fill that role. Sometimes one's own parents aren't the best ones to turn to — they don't always understand — Something as fragile and as precious as yourself should be protected." Mr. Springer's hand, still trembling, traveled slowly upward, toward Honey's thigh. "Will you promise me, Honey — that in such an event, you would feel free to come to me?"

"Oh, yes, thank you very much, Mr. Springer," Honey said. "Yes, I would. But I really can't wait any longer, now. I have to get the car back to Mother." She stood up; the hand fell away.

Mr. Springer sighed. Then he leaped to his feet, and escorted her to the door. "It has been so pleasant chatting with you," he said. "I shall tell Janet that you called. She will be so sorry to have missed you." He gave her a courtly bow.

"Good-bye, Mr. Springer," said Honey, "and thanks a lot for the lemonade. It was yummy."

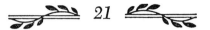

21

"IS THIS HONEY MCKITTRICK?"

"This is she speaking."

"Say, you may not know who I am, but I know who you are. I work at Meritt's service station. You were in the other day. I filled your dad's Buick up with gas. You recall a tall guy with wavy brown hair?"

"I seem to just sort of vaguely remember —"

"Well, I was wondering — by the way, the name is Curley Flint — I was wondering, see, if you'd care to go out for a beer some evening? We could drive down to the Stateline Club, maybe, and have a talk. I'd be interested in getting to know your philosophy of life."

"I don't drink beer."

"You can have a Coke, then. How about tomorrow night, around nine, when I get off work?"

"I could meet you at the station."

"Just ask for Curley."

"Okay," said Curley, after they were seated in the roadhouse booth, "let's have it. I want to know your philosophy."

"Well, I was thinking of helping the lepers, but —"

"The who?"

"The lepers."

"What lepers is that?"

"In India, maybe."

"Listen, take my advice. Forget the lepers. You have to LIVE. That's my philosophy. I'm going to live it up."

"Well, if you mean, have a good time, that's what I want, too."

"Good girl. Why don't you try a beer?"

"Well, I might. Just a little one."

"Did anyone ever tell you you weren't bad-looking?"

"Maybe."

"Who told you?"

"I couldn't say. It's a secret."

"Hey, you're a girl with secrets, huh? What other secrets you got?"

"I'll tell you one. I'm a monster, really."

"You're a what?"

"I lack a tragic sense of life. I'm a monster."

"You're a pretty funny kind of monster, if you ask me."

"Just the same, I am."

"Let's forget this monster thing, and get more serious. How about that beer?"

She tossed her head, so that a lock of hair fell over one eye; then she smiled up at Curley, beneath it. "I think I'll have a Tom Collins," she said.

 22

SUSANNA'S EXTRACURRICULAR ACTIVITY was on the high school annual, the *Modoc Chief.* At the end of the school year, she completed her contribution, which was entitled, "Pun My Word," and took up two full pages.

Strolling down Main Street the other day, we chanced to meet that famous oracle, Ching Chu Foo, who gave us the following forecast for the Class of '41 — in other words — the Class Prophecy!

Mary Reter — Gypsy Queen — A Mind Reter

Evajean Treece — Scrubwoman — Floor Flusher

Nathan Brenner — Printer — I like his "type"

Stella Burke — Vegetable dealer — she has "radish" hair and a "turn-up" nose

Teddy Lyons — Shipbuilder — at noon always out to launch

Vince Holbrook — Doctor — everything comes out all right

Buzzy Heffelfinger — Bandleader — he really has "sax" appeal

Honey McKittrick — Pastry maker — some cookie

Janet Springer — Music composer — "Oboe! Oboe!"

Harry Nakamura — Dentist — always makes a good impression

Susanna Swope — Author of Ghost stories —
written with invisible ink

Though she was secretly proud of her creations, she did not show them to Bennet.

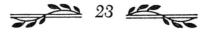 23

THE HIGH SCHOOL GYM had been transformed into a blue lagoon. Hundreds of tropical fish had been painted on butcher paper, which covered the walls. A mannequin loaned by Hinks Department Store, and dressed as a mermaid, was perched upon a papier-mâché rock. Next to the rock was an old leather trunk from the Springer attic, flowing over with costume jewelry. Kent Davids and his Local Aggregation were costumed as Davy Jones and his men; they played from a bandstand built to resemble an immense seashell. They played all the numbers which Glenn Miller and Benny Goodman and Tommy Dorsey had made popular.

"It is beautiful, if I do say so myself," said Janet, who was decorating chairman.

She was dancing with Buzzy Heffelfinger, president of the senior class, who had brought her. Everyone had assumed that Buzzy would ask Honey, and perhaps he had. But, one day, ever so matter-of-factly, Honey announced she was going with Wally Jones, who didn't even go to high school; he was a freshman, now, at the university, and had come down just to escort Honey to the prom.

Honey had arranged all of this without informing Janet or Susanna; yet, to Janet's annoyance, Susanna, when they discussed it, did not seem at all surprised.

"Well, this is certainly the end of an era in more ways than one," Janet had said to Susanna.

"It has been ending for some time."

"What do you mean?"

"Bennet Tidewater warned us."

"How can you listen to that pansy?" Janet said lightly, testing this disloyal observation upon Susanna.

But Susanna did not seem disconcerted. She said, "At any rate, perhaps it's the beginning, not the end."

"The beginning of — what?"

"We must wait and see."

"The thing is, it throws everything out of kilter.

I assumed Buzzy would go with Honey, and Nathan with you, and I would go with Vince. Isn't that what you assumed?"

"Assumptions can be dangerous."

"The question is, now what?"

"Can't you still go with Vince? He'll probably ask you."

"Vince has always preferred Honey," said Janet, stubbornly. "Perhaps it's just as well, in the long run. It will give him an opportunity not to invite me. But, we can't *not* go. We are princesses. I suppose I shall just have to accept whatever comes along."

"I was planning on doing that, myself."

"What if nothing does?" Janet said this as if it were a joke, to hide her panic.

"We could pretend to have measles."

"I've had measles."

"We can find an exotic disease."

"I do think Honey might have told us, earlier."

"Something has happened. Bennet Tidewater said that it would."

"Oh, please, shut up about him," Janet begged.

"Everything is all mixed up," said Janet to Buzzy, whom she had managed to meet, as if by accident, as he came out of chemistry class.

"How do you mean?"

"Well, you know, the prom."

"You mean, you aren't going with Vince?"

"Assumptions can be dangerous, nowadays."

"Well, then, you can come with me," he said, with a sudden grin.

"Thanks for your protective attitude."

"Don't be silly. The pleasure is all mine." He gave her a mock bow, then strutted off, down the hall.

Well, that would show Vince, thought Janet. It would show him she didn't have to always be Second Best. But, how ridiculous this was, because she was obviously Second Best, anyhow, with Buzzy. And why did she feel she had to show Vince anything? He had always been nice to her. The thing was, it was all Honey's fault. If Honey hadn't betrayed them first, nobody would be betraying anyone else, now. Nothing, she thought sincerely, was as sickening as betrayal.

"Well, this is certainly the end of an era," said Janet to Mrs. McKittrick, whom she managed to see alone, by dropping in when she knew Honey was having her hair done at the Fountain of Beauty.

"I know exactly what you mean," said Mrs. Mc-Kittrick. "I was thinking it myself. I think it's dreadful Honey is going to the prom with a stranger, and not one of the boys from her class. I

wanted to invite the young people for a late supper, afterwards, but the way things are now,
Honey says it won't work. I'm really terribly disappointed. I just read an article called 'Entertaining
for Teens,' I was going to make Dagwood sandwiches, that's what they're called."

"You could have your party anyhow," said Janet.

"Do you think I could? Honey says she won't
come."

"But it's *your* party. We come to see you, too."

"That's what I told the Doctor. I told him young
people like us. All right, perhaps I shall. I'll invite
you, first. And you tell Susanna."

"I'll help out," said Janet.

"Thank you, dear. That's more than I can say for
my own family."

The orchestra was playing "In the Mood."
Buzzy held Janet tightly against him, crushing her
gardenia corsage. Janet was slightly taller than he,
but this did not inhibit his dancing. He scooted all
over the floor; his green eyes turned glazed, as if he
were drunk. In a moment, she knew, he would
swing her out, as he was used to doing with
Honey, and she would be expected to execute a
series of steps by herself, at the same time moving
gradually toward him again. She could perform

this action by herself in her bedroom, but now the very thought of it made her stiff and clumsy.

"Think of yourself as a Queen, and Buzzy as your subject," she said quickly to herself. But there was not time. The moment was upon her. He dropped her hand; she missed the beat, and could not recover it. Buzzy had to scoot and shuffle the whole distance between them to retrieve her.

"Sorry," she said, "I was daydreaming."

He grinned and clutched her to him again, as if nothing had happened.

Then the orchestra began to play a slow, sad number, "Music, Maestro, Please." Good, thought Janet, this will give us a chance to talk. She gave a little push, trying to free herself from Buzzy's hug, but he only gripped her tighter. His ear was some-how below her mouth. She had never noticed a boy's ear much, before. It was so intimate-looking, somehow. Bare and downy. She felt trembly, look-ing at his ear.

"I am a Queen, and he is my subject," she said to herself in order to recover her composure. She crouched slightly, and directed her conversation into the orifice. "It's the absolute end, wouldn't you say?"

"What is?" said Buzzy.

"Our era. The Trio. You and Honey." She had to

shout above the music, so that it was difficult to keep a casual, chatty tone. "We're terribly worried about Honey, just now. Aren't you?"

"Huh?" Buzzy began to hum, under his breath to the music.

"I said we're all terribly worried about Honey."

"Why are we talking about Honey?" murmured Buzzy, in a teasing, sexy tone. He brushed his lips over her hair in a quieting gesture. Then he began to sing aloud. "For tonight, dum de dum, to-morrow —"

Dazed, she half recognized an opportunity; then she watched herself destroy it.

"What is your honest opinion of Wally Jones?"

"Can't say I have one." Suddenly, to her horror, he swung her out again. She did a few awkward steps, then, realizing she had been victimized, she froze — a prisoner in the middle of the dance floor.

"It's not a bad band," said Buzzy cheerfully, when he finally retrieved her, "only I wish they'd play more fast ones, don't you?"

Susanna had come with Vince, whom she knew would have preferred to escort Janet, though silly Janet did not seem to know this, and this knowledge gave her a relaxed, objective sort of attitude, which was the only attitude she cared to have with the opposite sex. Bennet's attempt at setting her hair had liberated her from any need to behave as society expected young girls to behave; she did not have to bother with coquetry or primping, which she now knew to be hopeless. She was free to observe, and she noted many things, which she wrote down afterwards in the notebook Bennet had suggested she keep; many writers did, he had told her. Her style, at first, was somewhat Victorian and didactic; later, it became more cryptic.

From Susanna's Notebook — Prom, 1941

Janet looked feverish. She called it the "End of an Era," but still clings desperately to the Past. She has spurned Bennet Tidewater, who is trying to lead her into the Future. Despite Janet, all of us Trio are becoming People in Our Own Right.

Honey glowed in her new, queenly beauty. She has a new way of tossing her head, so that a lock of dark hair falls over one eye. As she brushes it away, she smiles up at Wally Jones (her escort and perhaps a mere puppet to her present whims), in a most engaging Brenda Diana Duff Frazier manner. Bennet Tidewater says being beautiful is not easy.

Miss Henderson danced several dances with Mr. Masters, the football coach, talking all the time with extreme animation, while Miss Turknet, her wide shoulders looking misplaced and pathetic in

*a horrid mauve taffeta evening gown, sat glaring
upon the sidelines.*

*Nathan Brenner — surprise! surprise! — brought
Evajean Treece, the Poor Girl, whom Honey took
up, and then dropped, and who is said to have a
"reputation." By inviting Evajean, Nathan has set
himself off from safe society. He, too, is changing
and experimenting. Yes, change and experiment
were certainly the watchwords of this remarkable
evening.*

*Harry Nakamura, the son of the McKittricks'
gardener, and Valedictorian of our Class, brought
his younger sister, Mary Lou, who looked like a
fashion ad from Vogue.*

*We traded dances with Buzzy and Janet. Buzzy
has what Bennet Tidewater calls "grace." He is
aware that Something is Happening, and will ride
it out in his usual cheerful manner, enjoying the
Historical Moment as much as possible under the
circumstances.*

*Vince is more bewildered. He is one of the few
boys taller than Janet, and he appreciates her in-
telligence and good bony structure. When they
traded dances, they looked good together. But,
alas, it is not to be —*

*We traded dances with Teddy and the new girl,
Stella Marsh.*

"The old order changeth, yielding place to new."
And the Trio has fallen upon evil days. But why?
In what way?

None of us, I believe, wanted this to occur. But,
now, we cannot seem to stop it.

The dance had been in progress for about two hours, when, suddenly, the music stopped, and a path was cleared upon the dance floor. Then to the stately music of "Pomp and Circumstance," Queen Honey and her court, which consisted of Janet and Susanna and four other girls, entered the gym. They marched slowly, in a solemn procession, their pastel gowns sweeping the floor.

Honey was in pale blue, the color of her eyes. Her skin was flushed; her dark hair fell to her shoulders. On her head was a small gold-colored crown, embedded with paste jewels. She held her head high and looked neither to right nor to left.

Susanna wore pink; she walked a bit awkwardly; her straw-colored hair had been set at the Fountain of Beauty in too tight curls; occasionally she gave a quick, furtive glance about her; there was a tiny, impish grin upon her lips.

Janet wore green. Her hair was pulled up, off her face, in high curls, revealing her fine bony structure. She walked cautiously, careful to keep in step. The smell of floor wax and gardenias made her feel faint.

Buzzy, as president of the class of '41, was standing in the center of the gymnasium. As Honey reached him, he took her hand, and, holding it aloft, led her to the seashell throne in front of the bandstand; then he handed her her sceptre. After this, he bent down and kissed her lightly upon her cheek; she smiled gravely. Then he stepped to a mike; the music stopped, and he cried, "All Hail, Queen Honey!" The music continued; it soared to a crescendo; the audience broke out in cheers.

Dr. and Mrs. McKittrick, Mr. and Mrs. Heffelfinger, and Dr. and Mrs. Swope were sitting in the bleachers; they applauded proudly. Mrs. McKittrick had tears in her eyes. "It's the end of an era," she whispered to Dr. McKittrick.

"Well, they all have to end sometime," said the Doctor, patting her knee.

Bennet Tidewater, who had been practicing the organ late at the church that night, slipped into the gym for the coronation, and stood watching in the shadows.

Afterwards, everyone, except Honey and Wally Jones, went to the McKittricks for a late supper and more dancing.

Susanna wrote:

Outwardly, it was a most successful event, but I sensed a kind of pall hanging over the group, which they tried to dispel by frantic fun-making. What caused the pall? Absence of the daughter of the house? I believe it affected Dr. McKittrick and Buzzy Heffelfinger most of all. The Doctor was quieter than usual, and made fewer jokes, while Buzzy, on the other hand, danced wildly with Eva-jean Treece on the terrace.

Janet seemed happier, here, and spent her time helping Mrs. McKittrick serve the food. At two A.M., some of us went swimming.

While we were immersed, Honey appeared on the lawn, in all her regal finery. She had evidently said good-bye to her escort at the door. She looked beautiful and somewhat melancholy.

Janet, who was not in the pool, welcomed her as an important guest. Since she did not want to swim, we got out and dressed. Buzzy asked Honey to dance. But the pall seemed to deepen, and soon we all made our departure.

Was this a happy night for the Queen of our Prom? I wonder.

Everyone had left the McKittricks by three o'clock. Honey was in bed, in a half-dream. She was still a Queen. She sat upon her throne, but the throne room was empty of dancers and guests. The cleanup committee had stripped the walls and ceilings of decorations; the janitors, oblivious of her lofty station, were sweeping up. The room was transformed, again, into a bare gymnasium, smelling of sweat. In the crude morning light, her prom dress looked limp and fussy. She laid her sceptre across her knees.

"Just the same, I am Queen Honey," she said to herself. She picked up the sceptre, and stood up. "I am the Queen!" she announced in a loud voice, but, at that moment, the janitors began a dreadful din with their cleanup carts, and her voice was lost.

She sat up in bed. The din still continued, though she was sure she was now fully awake. Someone was throwing pebbles at her window. She got up and looked out. In the dawn light, a shadowy figure stood upon the lawn, beside the pool. It was Buzzy.

"For Pete's sakes," she whispered, "what do you want?"

"Come on," whispered Buzzy back, "let's drive out to the river. Bring your suit."

They reached Possum Bridge just as the sun was rising. The river flowed swiftly beneath the old covered bridge; here and there a rock produced a riffle — a baroque swirl, surrounded by leaping spray. They got out of the car and walked across the bridge, which was closed now to automobile traffic. Sunlight shot through holes in the roof, illuminating the dark interior. The noise of their feet on the old boards echoed in the rafters. Beneath them, through a crack in the floor, the water roared.

They put on their suits on the other side; then they threw themselves into the cold current, which carried them under the bridge, and out to the middle of the river. Here they struck out, and broke through the current; then they swam to the opposite shore. Exhausted and exhilarated, they threw themselves down upon the iron-colored, brackish-smelling sand.

"There's an elephant buried there, under that bridge support," said Buzzy, when they got their breath.

"An elephant?"

"Really. My dad told me. A circus came to town, one day, years ago, and an elephant got sick and died, and they brought him out here, and buried him."

"Janet's father should know that," said Honey. "He could put it in his History."

"Speaking of history, Janet says it's the end of an era. She says the Trio is no more."

"Janet can be, well — difficult sometimes. I suppose it's because she has brains. She thinks I'm a monster at the moment. My mother does, too. I guess I am, sort of."

"You're not a monster," Buzzy said.

Honey tossed her head, so that a lock of damp hair fell over one eye; she pushed it back languidly and smiled up at Buzzy. "That's really terribly sweet of you, Buzzy," she said.

Buzzy grinned and stood up. He held out his hand and pulled Honey to her feet. He took her in his arms. She stood there, limply, while he kissed her once, very gently, upon her mouth. She held her face toward him, waiting for more, but he turned very quickly away.

"Time for the New Era to begin," he cried. "Come on, march! March! March! To the beat of the drum of the New Era! Out with the Old! On with the New! Into the Future! March to the drum!"

And they marched, in single file, back across the bridge to get their clothes, the rafters echoing to the noise of their tramping feet.

When they had dressed and returned to the car, they found Arthur, asleep in the back seat. This struck them as the funniest thing that had happened, ever. Even years later, when one of them brought it up, they would laugh, hysterically.

ALTHOUGH THE TRIO'S SPIRITUAL BOND had weakened, owing to treacheries, they were still known as the Trio, even in such far distant places as the university. Before Rush Week began, word had reached the sororities that to pledge one of the Trio, one had to pledge them all.

Despite this, you will be pledging three individuals, wrote Miss Henderson to her old sorority. *You will obtain an Activity Girl (Janet Springer), a Scholar (Susanna Swope), and a Date Girl (Honey McKittrick).*

So it was that the Trio, who might have preferred separate identities, found themselves all members of Pi Beta Phi.

Janet plunged into clubs and committees, and Pi Beta Phi was very pleased to have this on their record. One of the senior activity girls, who was president of the Girls' League, planned to groom her to be a BWOC (Big Woman on Campus).

Susanna studied and got good grades. She took Plato and Latin and English literature and music appreciation and geology. Yet none of these courses really excited her. What she enjoyed most of all was her extracurricular work on the *Oregon Emerald,* the school newspaper. After a few weeks of doing odd jobs in the office, her hard work and talent were recognized, and she was permitted to write a column, entitled "Under the Ivy," with her own by-line.

What professor is sporting a new goatee, and we wonder why? Could it be that he wants to look like G. B. Shaw, his favorite author?

Has anyone noticed the new art prints in the Reading Room at the Libe? This bright idea was Janet Springer's, who is Chairwoman of the Friends of the Library.

What Pi Beta Phi nugget is dating both a Phi Delt and a Beta at the same time? Remember boys, there's a law against dueling!

Our new Frosh Prexy, Buzzy Heffelfinger, is sporting a letter in Track, which ought to serve him well running away from his many female admirers.

Vince Holbrook and Teddy Lyons went home to Norton over Thanksgiving. The rumor was that they almost didn't return, owing to hangovers from quote eating too much turkey unquote.

Early Sunday mornings, Susanna would slip down to the lounge, where girls and boys had sat on old sofas in the darkness the night before, listening to records and necking. She would lift up the loose pillows on the sofas and collect the change which had fallen out of the boys' pockets. She usually found at least a dollar, sometimes two or three.

Honey started to date freshman boys, and soon graduated to seniors. She wore an I.D. bracelet belonging to a Sigma Nu who had joined the service, and a Phi Delt pin at night, on her nightgown, over her heart.

Sometimes, on Sunday afternoons, Vince and Buzzy and Teddy Lyons came over and took the Trio on a picnic, or to a movie. They would tease Honey, asking her which boy she was going steady with today, and she would smile mysteriously.

On Sunday evenings, Susanna would write to Bennet about college life.

We form a circle and close our eyes and sing a horrible song, at the end of which, we press one another's hands. It is sickening.

Date girls are revered the highest, next come Activity Girls, Scholars last. Well, no doubt, that is the way of the world. I am not a real scholar any-

how. I don't listen to the contents of the lectures so much as observe the lecturer.

We are going to be initiated and find out what Pi Beta Phi means. You are not supposed to tell anyone, or even say the word aloud. . . .

We were initiated last week. We were kept in our rooms for hours; then someone came for us, one by one. We were blindfolded and led downstairs to the secret basement chapter room, which smelled of incense. They told us the secret meaning of Pi Beta Phi, which is "True, Tried Friend," and is never supposed to be spoken aloud. When the blindfolds were removed we saw that a number of older alumni, including my mother and Miss Henderson, had come for the occasion. Miss Henderson wept and kissed us.

It was all quite disappointing to the three of us, who, as members of the Trio, understand the meaning of friendship — its glories and vicissitudes. Janet, owing to her status as an Activity Girl, was forced to be serious, but Honey giggled out loud. We all met the next day on campus, and, in a cloistered area, shouted "True, Tried Friend" — then burst into hysterical giggles.

I cannot imagine our lasting four years in this environment. Yet everyone, including our parents,

consider us fortunate to be here, among the chosen.
Perhaps being in the Trio spoiled us.
  I am reading Milton in English Lit.

> *"Farewell, happy fields,*
> *Where joy forever dwells! Hail, hor-*
>   *rors! hail,*
> *Infernal world! and thou, profoundest*
>   *Hell . . ."*

Does this not remind you of the Trio, who have
been, through their own doing, expelled from Para-
dise, and yet will always be plagued by its memory?

Bennet would write back, apologizing because
his letters were intended for all three girls:

I should address each one of you individually, as
you are now working out your individual destinies.
But, alas, Time does not permit me to do so at the
moment.
  Susanna, being a writer, has kept me informed,
though her descriptions of campus life are apt to
be careless and vague. "It is sickening," Susanna,
explains little, other than your own very subjective
and imprecatory reaction to sorority ritual. Try
harder, please.
  I understand that Janet is making a name for

herself in Activities. This is admirable, Janet, if you do not permit Busy Work to substitute for your Spiritual Life, nor Ambition to take the place of Love, Honor and Loyalty. The same holds true for Honey and Society.

These are evil times. I am firmly convinced we shall have to go to war to defeat Herr Hitler and am engrossed, at present, in trying to find a way to serve my country. The Air Force is not interested in me because of my myopia. I shall try the Navy next. The difficult part will be leaving my mother. Pray for the Allied Cause.

Yours sincerely,

Bennet Tidewater

25

ONE SUNDAY MORNING in early December, Susanna and Janet went to church; then, upon their return they trooped up to Honey's room to interrogate her about the Phi Delt dance she had attended the night before.

Honey was still in bed — the props of the dance scattered about her. A crumpled gardenia corsage on the floor gave off a hothouse sweetness. Her green chiffon formal hung over a chair. A new dance program was wedged into her mirror. Her bedside radio was on low, and Frankie was singing, "All or Nothing at All."

Janet and Susanna drew up chairs about her bed.

"Tell us about the dance," said Janet.

"The dance?" Honey's voice was muffled and sleepy. "Oh, it was lovely." She began to hum along with Frankie.

"Tell us about the decorations," said Janet.

" 'Moonlight cocktail.' That was the theme. Everything was bluish and moonlighty."

"Have you decided, are you in love with him?" Janet nodded toward the Phi Delt pin Honey wore upon her nightgown.

"Oh, heavens, no, but he's a darling."

"Then it's the other one, the Sigma Nu," Janet said. "You're in love with him."

"With who?" said Honey.

"With whom," corrected Susanna.

Honey giggled and burrowed under the covers. "He's terribly sweet," she said, her voice sounding faraway.

The music on the radio suddenly stopped and a man's voice — rapid and high-pitched — replaced it. "Bulletin — Japanese — Pearl Harbor."

"To tell you the truth," said Honey, popping up again —

"The President of the United States is —"

"There is somebody. Somebody brand-new." The voice on the radio interrupted her thoughts, and she reached over lazily and flicked it off.

"Someone else?" said Janet, eagerly.

"I met him last night. He's already graduated and he's an ensign in the navy in San Diego. He came back for his old fraternity dance. You should see him in his uniform, all white and gold. His name is Jack Parsons."

"What Parsons is that?" said Susanna.

"No Parsons we know. He's from Portland."

"A Mysterious Stranger," Susanna said.

Honey laughed — a happy, private little laugh. "He's absolutely divinely dreamy," she said. Then, as if she needed to savor this statement alone, she disappeared under the covers again.

"Does he like you?" said Janet, standing up, and talking down to the hump in the bed.

There was no answer, but the blankets quivered from Honey's laughter.

"Honey, please come out. We want to know if this is serious," Janet said in a severe tone. "After all, we are the Trio. You wouldn't want others to know, first."

"I think it might be serious," said a muffled voice.

Susanna went over to the radio and snapped it back on. The voice was saying, " — therefore, officially at war."

"I think something has happened," Susanna said.

Honey sat bolt upright in bed. "Something extremely important *has* happened," she said, with a grin.

26

THE WAR, which had begun that morning in Honey's room, and which she had flicked off, nevertheless continued, and when, in a few days, everyone had got over the initial shock, Honey provided another one by announcing, secretly, to her parents and to the Trio, that she was engaged to Jack Parsons.

"What Parsons is that?" said Mrs. McKittrick, when she had somewhat recovered.

"No Parsons we know," said Honey. "A Portland

Parsons." She tossed her head, and smiled dreamily. If anything, her romance had made her more beautiful.

"I shall have to talk to this young man," said Dr. McKittrick.

"You are much much too young and marriage is forever," Mrs. McKittrick said. Nevertheless, she planned a wedding in her mind. Navy blue and royal gold? Royal gold and forest green? Chartreuse and lemon yellow? She hoped she would have no silly problems with Honey about wearing a traditional white gown, as some mothers these days had.

27

HONEY WAS YOUNG, but it was wartime, and Jack Parsons would have to go overseas anytime. Somehow, before anyone quite realized what was happening, Mrs. McKittrick had invited close friends to a luncheon.

Janet helped with the decorations. Pink and gold were the colors they chose. Cupid's colors. The tablecloth was pink, they used Mrs. McKittrick's white china, rimmed with gold. The centerpiece was a three-tiered dish, filled with tiny apples, sprayed with gold paint. "Love apples," Mrs. McKittrick called them. At each place was a tiny pink card in the shape of a heart, with the names Honey and Jack written upon them.

"It is pretty, if I do say so myself," Mrs. McKittrick said, surveying the table.

"It's a masterpiece," said Janet.

Mrs. McKittrick had invited Janet and Susanna's mothers; two aunts; an elderly cousin of Dr. McKittrick's; Miss Henderson; shy, mousy little Mrs. Tidewater; Mrs. Heffelfinger; Mrs. Lyons; Mrs. Collier; and the new girl, Stella Marsh, whom the Trio had "discovered" the summer before. Together, Janet and Mrs. McKittrick decided not to invite Evajean Treece. They felt she would not be comfortable.

As the ladies sat down to the table and read the pink cards, there were shrieks of delighted surprise. Susanna and Janet exchanged glances.

"For heaven's sakes, Jack *Who* —? I can't bear it!" cried Miss Henderson.

"He's a Portland Parsons," Mrs. McKittrick explained.

"How long have they known each other?" asked the elderly cousin.

"Things are different in wartime," Mrs. McKittrick said.

"He's an absolute darling," said Janet. "Both Susanna and I are madly in love with him."

"Anyone Honey would choose would have to be special," Susanna found herself saying. She felt this was expected of her, as a member of the Trio. Whereupon, immediately, she made a private vow never to say such meaningless things again. Her eccentricity, after this, came into full flower.

 28

AFTER THE LUNCHEON, Honey went to her room to rest before she went out that evening with Jack Parsons, who was down for the weekend, and who, during the luncheon, had been put into Dr. McKittrick's custody.

Susanna and Janet lingered on, helping Mrs. McKittrick and the maid clean up.

"It was a beautiful luncheon, if I do say so, myself," said Mrs. McKittrick.

"It was scrumptious," said Janet.

Then she and Susanna walked over to Susanna's house. The house was empty; Susanna's mother had gone from the luncheon to a meeting of the Eastern Star.

They sat down at the kitchen table. Susanna slipped off her high heels under the table; Janet played with her white gloves in her lap.

"Well, what do you think?" said Janet, after a moment.

"Bennet Tidewater said something was bound to happen."

"Anyone can say that. What I'm interested in is the psychology in back of it all. For instance, *why* is Honey escaping into Jack Parsons's arms?"

"I never thought of her 'escaping,'" said Susanna. "What does she have to escape from?"

"From Life, of course. You don't happen to have any cigarettes around here, do you?"

"Nobody smokes." Then Susanna remembered the ancient pack of Camels she had stolen, years ago, from Dr. McKittrick.

"There might be some in my room," she said. Janet followed her upstairs. Susanna rummaged in a bottom drawer and found the cigarettes.

While they were gone, Roger entered the kitchen. He took a dollar bill from Janet's purse, and then slipped out again.

The girls went back downstairs. Janet lit a cigarette, coughed, made a face, then went on smoking. "Obviously, college means nothing to Honey," she said. "Not for an education, that is. It was just a happy hunting ground for a man, and she grabbed the first presentable one that came along."

"Oh, she's always had boyfriends," said Susanna. "And she and Jack Parsons look well together, don't you think? He's extremely handsome."

"Susanna, I would expect more depth from you," said Janet.

"Everyone thinks people who aren't pretty or popular with boys are deep," Susanna said. "This is a fallacy. I'm actually rather shallow."

"But *you* want more to your life than just marriage and housekeeping. Ugh. And babies? I always thought the Trio had High Ambitions. Now, Honey has failed us. The fact is, she's weak."

"She's in love," said Susanna. Never having been in love herself, she accepted the phenomenon without question.

"But there is love and love. Love is fine, if it makes you grow, if you don't use it to hide from life. I personally, don't intend to just say to a man, here, take care of me, I'm yours, forever, as if you're some sort of parcel. I intend to express my own personality, not just hide in the shadow of a man."

"What sort of a man would you like if you could choose?" said Susanna, who was genuinely curious.

"A doctor, I think. I can see myself as a doctor's wife. He will serve humanity and I would support

him. We would explore life together, as . . . part-
ners."

"Like the McKittricks?"

"I would do more for my husband than Mrs. Mc-
Kittrick does for hers. I'm speaking psychologi-
cally, of course. By the way, do you know what
Jack and Honey are going to do tomorrow?"

"What?"

"They're going to look at household appliances."

"Oh."

"Can't you just see them, going into Gidol's,
hand in hand, and examining waffle irons. Doesn't
it make you sick?"

They looked uneasily at one another across the
table; then they both fell silent. Marriage, to them
was still another world — far distant, and scarcely
real — like old age. Yet Honey was about to enter
this world. She would enter it and shut the door
and pull down the blinds, and they would never
know her again — not, at least as they had known
her. She might as well be entering a nunnery as far
as the two remaining members of the Trio were
concerned.

"These ciggies are stale," said Janet, after a moment.

"They've been around for a while," said Susanna.

29

THE WEDDING WAS TO BE HELD just after Christmas. One day, during the holidays, Janet dropped over to the McKittricks, and found Jack Parsons in the living room, alone. That morning he and Honey had had their photograph taken, and he was still wearing his naval ensign's uniform. He was so handsome that Janet, who prided herself on not being "taken in by mere looks," stared at him in wonder.

"Honey and her mother are downtown shopping for stuff," Jack Parsons said. "I expect them back, any moment, but you know how ladies are when they get into stores."

"I'll just wait a bit, anyhow," said Janet. "Do you happen to have a cigarette?"

Jack Parsons gave her one, and lit it for her. She sat across from where he had been sitting, but Jack remained standing, smiling down at her.

"I've been hoping to get a chance to see you alone, anyhow," she said. Jack Parsons did not say anything, so she went on. "I've been dying to tell you how pleased we are that Honey chose you."

"I have always thought of it as my privilege," said Jack Parsons.

"I don't think we could have stood it, for example, if she had married that horrible Sigma Nu."

"We?" said Jack Parsons, curiously.

"I'm speaking, of course, of the Trio. What's left of it, that is. Susanna and me."

"I see."

"Honey needed the security of marriage, she's not really the Higher Education type, as you may have noticed, so, thank God, you came along just in time."

"I second that," said Jack Parsons.

"She needs a mature person, she's had such a sheltered life."

"More than you?" said Jack Parsons, with his nice smile.

"Heavens, yes. Everything has been so easy for Honey, she's only had to reach out for something and there it is. She doesn't have the slightest notion what Real Life is about."

"I'm not sure I do, either. Do you?"

"I've been exposed to more — vicissitudes. It has a maturing effect."

"I find this all extremely interesting," Jack Parsons said. "I mean Norton and the Trio and all. Tell me something, do you know Bennet Tidewater?"

Janet uttered a short, derisive laugh. "Heavens, yes."

"Tell me about him."

"What is there to tell? He's a fairy."

"Besides that."

"Isn't that enough?"

"Tell me about the Trio then."

"Honey must have told you about us."

"I'd like to hear it from you, too."

"What would you like to know?"

"Well, sometimes, I feel slightly — apologetic — for breaking it up."

"Oh, you're not really breaking it up," said Janet, staunchly. "I mean, in a way, you'll be marrying the Trio, too."

"I see. Well, it's nice to know."

"Yes. You'll find me the most reliable member in — in emergencies. Please call upon me, any time."

"It's very kind of you, and I'll remember that," Jack Parsons said.

30

HONEY WAS MARRIED just after Christmas. It was a beautiful wedding, everyone said so.

"It was a beautiful wedding," Mrs. McKittrick sighed.

Janet had helped her choose the decor. Avocado green gowns for the two bridesmaids (there was no maid of honor, as it would have been impossible to choose); forest green embankments of foliage, tied with lime green ribbons; gold candles; the bride, in white, leaning lightly upon Dr. McKittrick's arm.

When Jack Parsons stepped forward to claim her, a hush fell over the guests: two such handsome young people stirred everyone. Then Honey tossed her head, so that a lock of dark hair fell over one eye, and, looking up at her bridegroom, smiled mysteriously.

"I could have died," said Janet, afterwards, to Susanna.

31

BUT NOW THE WEDDING was over. And Honey was
gone. She and Jack were living in San Diego at the
navy base. The McKittrick home, so recently filled
with Honey's friends and admirers, sprawling on
the sofas, dancing in the darkened living room,
swimming in the pool, eating Mrs. McKittrick's
good food, drinking Dr. McKittrick's liquor, had
an air of suspended life.

Mrs. McKittrick began to develop strange com-
pulsive habits. Two or three times a day she would
wander up to Honey's room, carrying some object
— a wedding present that had arrived late,
Honey's tennis racket, her set of golf clubs, an old
high school annual, which she thought Honey
might want in her new home — and add it to the
growing pile upon the bed.

Before she left, she would glance around — at
Honey's dance programs stuck in the mirror, at the
collection of stuffed animals on the bed — or she
would open a drawer, and pore over photographs
of Honey's old beaux, or peer into the closet at the

assortment of leftover clothes — a pair of run-down tennis shoes, an old formal, a ruffled petti-coat. Then she would sigh gently and go out and close the door.

Things went on like this for a month, until spring vacation at the university. Now, toward evening, Mrs. McKittrick grew especially appre-hensive. She rushed outdoors and gathered flowers in the dusk and arranged them in silver bowls in the living room; she put on fresh lipstick and per-fume, and, though Dr. McKittrick urged her, she could not settle down to a game of gin rummy.

Then, one evening, the doorbell rang; Mrs. Mc-Kittrick's eyes brightened, and her mouth lost its aging, droopy look; she scuttled across the room to the front door.

"Why, hello, there," she cried, to Janet and Su-sanna and Buzzy and Teddy and Vince. "Why, hello there, come on in!"

They filed in like automatons. It was as if they were somehow bound to the McKittricks, forever, even though the old tie had now been severed.

"Look who's here!" Mrs. McKittrick said to the Doctor.

"Well, well, well, what do you know?" the Doc-tor said. He was pleased, not only for himself, but for his wife. "Can I buy you all a drink?" he said to them.

They all trooped out to the kitchen, and, after admiring Mrs. McKittrick's new burnt orange lino- leum — "No, it was not too loud, it was just right" — and being shown her recently acquired antique dry sink — "I see we have more money in the bank," said the Doctor — they fixed themselves rum and Coca-Colas and took them out to the patio.

Mrs. McKittrick remained in the kitchen — emerging, after a few minutes, with a bowl of guacamole dip.

"I hope I haven't missed anything," she cried.

"We're talking about the wedding," said Janet.

"It was a beautiful wedding, if I do say so my- self!"

"If you don't, who will?" laughed the Doctor.

"Everyone says so. People stop me on the street just to tell me."

"It was terrific," said Buzzy.

"We think he's great," Janet said.

"Who?" said Mrs. McKittrick.

"Jack Parsons!"

"Well, if you think *I* don't think he's a dear —" said Mrs. McKittrick.

"We all approve," said Teddy.

Susanna said, "He looks as though he will be kind to her, but —"

"Kind!" exclaimed Mrs. McKittrick. "He's the

kindest, sweetest, most thoughtful young man. He sent me roses, while they were on their honeymoon. He thanked me for the beautiful, beautiful wedding."

"Of course one never knows," Susanna finished.

"One never knows what?" said Mrs. McKittrick. The drink and excitement had gone to her head.

"Whether or not people will be kind."

"Well, I know. He's kind, all right. He better be," Mrs. McKittrick said.

"Well, it's time for an old man to get his beauty rest," said Dr. McKittrick. He stood up. "Don't let me stop the party. See you in the spring."

"She forgot her tennis racket, I'll have to send it to her," Mrs. McKittrick said. "By the way, the pictures came. You girls look adorable. And there's a sweet one of Buzzy toasting the bride."

"Old Buzz was crocked," said Teddy.

"I was not."

"He threw up, afterwards, at the club."

"I had flu."

"That's a good name for it."

"Presents are still arriving," said Mrs. McKittrick. "I had no idea people could be so marvelous. I'll have to bundle everything up and put in her tennis racket, too."

Susanna got up to say good-bye; it was late and she was feeling oddly depressed, as if they were all participating in Honey's wake. But Mrs. McKittrick would not hear of her going.

"Everyone must have one more drink," she cried.

Then Buzzy stood up. "I'll fix them for you, Althea," he said, using Mrs. McKittrick's first name for the first time. He did it consciously in order to please her, and unconsciously, because he suddenly felt old.

"Althea will have a rum and cola," Mrs. McKittrick said with a giggle.

"Althea is such a romantic name," said Janet.

"Do you think so?" Mrs. McKittrick said. "I always thought it was dreadfully old-fashioned."

"It seems modern, somehow."

"Do you really think so? It's terribly sweet of you to say so," Mrs. McKittrick said.

After this, they came often, whenever they were home on weekends. But things were not the same. Though they went through the same gestures — joking, eating, drinking Dr. McKittrick's liquor, admiring Mrs. McKittrick's new decors — their laughter seemed hollow and forced; their conversations drifted aimlessly away like their cigarette smoke in the warm nights.

"You see, they come to see us, not just Honey," Mrs. McKittrick told the Doctor.

But it was as if she were trying to convince herself.

 32

WHENEVER SUSANNA CAME HOME, she visited Bennet in his room. He would play chamber music for her on his phonograph or read to her from John Donne or T. S. Eliot. Susanna had no taste for any of this, but Bennet's deep, sonorous voice and the trappings of his room gave her the feeling of being on some distant, exotic shore, far from the Pi Phi house.

He also continued to give her lessons in Observation.

"Describe the Farmers and Merchants Bank."

"Well, there is a clock, and old men stand under it, and sometimes the Salvation Army. It is big and marbly."

"You can't just say, marbly. Besides, it isn't all. Describe the Hotel Jackson."

"Potted palms, a tile floor, big leather chairs, lamps with fringes, a cigar counter; a masculine atmosphere, except on Sundays, when old ladies eat dinner there."

"Better. Describe the Natatorium. Now, take your time."

"The Natatorium." She shut her eyes, then opened them. "An immense, hot, moist, echoing, sulphur-smelling wooden palace which encloses a rectangular swimming tank. The ceiling, above the tank, culminates in a Byzantine dome, in which is set a green skylight, covered with chicken wire. Over the deep end are trapezes. On the left side of the tank are dressing rooms — wooden cubicles with a cement floor, always awash with lukewarm water. A cement walk surrounds the pool. There are two black hands. One says MEN, another LADIES. They point to the dressing rooms. Other signs say, SWIM AT YOUR OWN RISK, PLEASE DO NOT EXPECTORATE IN POOL, and SUITS AND TOWELS FOR RENT."

"Describe the river, at Possum Bridge."

"The river is a green god."

"Stop! You were doing so nicely. What in heaven's name do you mean by saying the river is a green god? Do you really believe that?"

"No."

"The river is a river. God is God. One God, Creator of heaven and earth. God created the river, so how can He *be* the river? Try again."

"The river is swift and green at Possum Bridge."

"That's better," said Bennett, "though it's only the right way for everyone to express himself. Proper, accurate language, first, then divine inspiration. I'm afraid I can't help you with the latter. It's a question of grace."

 33

"IF I SPEAK to you openly as a mature woman speaks to another mature woman, it is because I can no longer consider you a schoolgirl," said Miss Henderson, whom Janet now called Henny, to Janet.

They sat in Henny's and Turky's apartment — their shoes off, their feet up on a coffee table, sipping sherry and smoking. "There is your sensitivity, for example," Henny went on. "That must be cultivated. It must not be left to harden and grow cold and dead, as has happened to Turky. Take A. A. Milne. She calls it childish because I enjoy reading *Winnie-the-Pooh*."

> *Isn't it funny, how a bee likes honey;*
> *Buzz buzz buzz, I wonder why he does —*

quoted Janet.

"Exactly," Henny said. She sighed heavily. "You have no idea how rare it is to find another human being on this earth with whom I can communicate. This town stifles me."

"Norton is not the world," quoted Janet.

"Exactly. If it weren't for this War I think I just might pick up and go to Morocco, or the Far East. Wouldn't that surprise bossy old Turky? Did you know she made me paint this apartment this vile, bilious green? It makes me ill, positively. But you have to compromise somewhere. And she gossips. I happen to know she has said things about us. Yes, my dear, you and me. She's madly jealous."

"What does she say?"

"She says that all the members of the Trio are spoiled vapid little girls, and that you are the most conceited of all. I told her that might have been true in the days when the Trio was together, but now that the Trio was no more — that you had matured, immensely."

"I'm trying," said Janet, sincerely. "I do try. But I wouldn't go so far as to say the Trio is no more. Honey is gone, of course. And Susanna and I — are different."

"You can say that again."

"Without Honey, you see, our differences seem — greater. But the Trio — there's still *something* — it's hard to explain."

" 'The old order changeth, yielding place to new,' Alfred Lord. By the way, do you know the nineteenth century English poets?"

"I haven't read a lot, actually," said Janet. "My mother does. I suppose she forced it on me too early. I've always envied Susanna's literary talent."

"It depends on what you mean by talent. I would be more apt to call Susanna's a 'skill.' She has built a wall around herself, I fear. No true artist lives behind a wall or in an ivory tower. You have to reach out. Art is a religion, a communication, not an escape."

"I was meaning to tell you — I was thinking, myself, of leaving Norton. My parents can't afford to send me to the university, anymore. I was thinking of going to Los Angeles, maybe, and finding a job. Do you think I'm mature enough?"

"If it's because Los Angeles is near Honey, then you aren't mature enough," Henny said.

"Well, San Francisco, then," said Janet.

"I was thinking, quite frankly, of doing the same thing, myself, particularly after what Turky said last night."

"What did she say?"

"She accused me of making a play for Mr. Masters at the senior prom. As if I haven't had enough of coaches!"

"Have you ever thought of marrying?" said Janet, boldly.

"My dear! Everyone *thinks* of it. To actually do it is quite another thing."

"But was there — ever — anyone special?"

"Did you know that Mr. Masters is going into the army — as an athletic director? Well, let him go. The army is the right spot for him. To each his own, I always say. Here, read this aloud, while I pour some more wine. Read the part about Eeyore losing his tail."

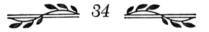 34

IT WAS SUMMER. The mountains had turned into lavender shadows; toward afternoon, the sun was a round ball of flame in the hazy sky. The pear blossoms were gone; the pears were growing fat and brown. The town was filled with transient workers and little barefoot boys, who hopped from shady spot to shady spot on the hot pavement.

Buzzy and Vince had both enlisted in the marines and were working in the mill until they received their orders. Nathan Brenner was a member of ASTP at Stanford. Bennet Tidewater, rejected by the army air corps and navy, was waiting to hear from the army signal corps. In the meantime he practiced making signals from two flags he had made. He would spell out strange phrases.

"Damn the torpedoes. Full speed ahead."

"Once more unto the breach, dear friends, once more."

"Theirs not to reason why, theirs but to do and die."

"It is different from other summers," said Janet.

She was working at Hinks Department Store in interior decoration. When ladies came in to look at samples of curtain or upholstery material, they were referred to Janet, as someone who had a "natural color sense." This meant that she never called a color merely "red" or "brown"; her colors were far more intriguing. They were "Mexican pink," or "avocado green" or "marine blue," or "deep-water aqua." The customers made their purchases and returned again; the department took on a new glamour. The manager of that floor began to refer to Janet's job as a "position."

Susanna worked as a copy girl at the *News Sentinel,* replacing people who were on summer vacations. She did odd jobs, learned to write headlines, and was in charge of "Locals and Personals." That summer, Susanna's acquaintances became newspaper celebrities.

Miss Louise Henderson, English teacher at Norton High School, is spending a week in San Francisco, sampling city life, and soaking up culture.

She did not add, as she could have, "along with Mr. Hal Masters, well-known coach at Norton High."

Mr. Theodore Lyons, recent Norton High School graduate, who has completed his Freshman year at the University of Oregon, has left for Quantico to begin his training in the United States Marine Corps.

Mrs. Rudolph Swope, wife of Dr. Rudolph Swope, well-known Norton dentist, has left for Corvallis, Oregon, where she will attend the State Convention of the Daughters of the Eastern Star. Mrs. Swope is a local Conductress of that esteemed organization.

Miss Maribell Turknet, teacher of Physical Education at Norton High School, has just entered the Women's Auxiliary Army Corps, where she will take officer training. Salutes, Miss Turknet.

She did not add, as she could have, that Miss Turknet had become estranged from her longtime roommate, Miss Louise Henderson, of the Cargill Court Apartments.

Janet and Susanna met for lunch at Melter's Creamery, which was patronized by working people. They sat at the counter, along with the office girls and clerks and stenographers, and drank plain Cokes and ate egg sandwiches and smoked cigarettes. They wore high heels but their legs were bare, on account of Japan, and their manner was brisker.

"Have you heard from Honey?" said Susanna.

"Of course not. She scarcely writes her own family."

During the first month after Honey and Jack Parsons's honeymoon, Janet and Susanna both received regular chatty letters from Mrs. Jack Parsons, in which she regaled them with amusing tales of domestic horrors — Jell-O that would not set, shrinking Jack's favorite civilian argyle socks, a first dinner party to which she invited Jack's commanding officer, and then failed to time the roast properly, so that we had to "drink cocktails until ten."

But as Honey settled into her new life, the letters dropped off. The Jell-O evidently set now; the socks no longer shrank, the roasts came out on time. Now that she could no longer share these first adventures at housekeeping with her friends, what was there left for her to share? This, even more than the wedding, seemed a cutting-off point.

"Perhaps there is trouble," said Janet to Susanna.

"Trouble?"

"Most new couples have difficulty making an adjustment. I am speaking, of course, of sex. I should think Honey might have difficulties that way, don't you?"

To Susanna, the idea of going to bed, of sleeping and waking up with a strange man — a Portland Parsons — was so beyond her imagination that the fact that Honey had attempted this made her assume she would succeed.

"Marriage is not a bed of roses," said Janet. "Henny and I have discussed this. Sexual incompatibility is very common — more common than you would guess."

"I have never been sure what sexual incompatibility means."

"Oh, Susanna!"

"Anyway, Bennet Tidewater says marriage is more than just sex."

"It would have to be, for him."

"He doesn't discount it. He says sex is a physical symbol for spiritual union."

"I can't really spend my time in discussing what Bennet Tidewater thinks about sex. I have a customer coming in to look at carpets. Here's my money. I have to dash."

35

ONE DAY IN LATE AUGUST a surprising thing happened. With absolutely no announcement of her plans, Honey drove up in the McKittrick driveway in the Ford convertible Dr. McKittrick had given the young couple for a wedding present and told her mother she had come to pay a visit. She looked very beautiful, but thin and pale, and when Mrs. McKittrick asked her nervously if everything was all right, she said, of course, why shouldn't it be, crossly.

At first, Mrs. McKittrick almost went out of her mind with joy. She ran to the phone and called Dr. McKittrick.

"Guess who's here?" she said. When he couldn't guess, she said, "Honey!"

"Honey?" said Dr. McKittrick. "Jack, too?"

"Jack? No, not Jack."

"Where is Jack?"

"I don't know. I didn't think to ask her."

"How long is she staying?"

"I don't know. I didn't ask her that, either. Her room isn't ready, though — I better go. If she'd only let me know, I would have had her room ready."

When Honey followed her mother up to her room, she stopped in the doorway with a bewildered look. The wedding presents were still piled all over the bed, but numerous other household objects — an extra ironing board, a rolled-up rug, some picture frames — had been pushed into the room, Mrs. McKittrick having discovered it made an excellent storage space.

"Naturally, we'll always keep your room for you," Mrs. McKittrick said, "only — I had no idea — This has been such a surprise. Such a pleasant surprise, naturally —" She felt dimly she had committed some crime against her own blood, that she had betrayed her daughter in her absence.

But Honey just took the wedding gifts and piled them into a corner of the room and threw her overnight case on the bed.

"How is Jack?" said Mrs. McKittrick timidly. She felt suddenly shy when she thought about this strange, handsome young man who was now her son-in-law.

"Jack? He's fine." The way Honey answered her did not encourage further conversation along these lines.

While Honey was lying down for a nap, Mrs. Mc-Kittrick telephoned Janet.

"Guess who's here?" she said.

There was a silence, and then Janet said, "Honey?"

"How did you know?"

"It's just a feeling I have. Is Jack with her?"

"No."

"I see."

"Do you think anything has — happened?" Mrs. McKittrick said, nervously. "I don't like to ask. She seems so touchy."

"We must wait and see. I'll be over tonight."

"I was hoping you would come, it would make me feel more comfortable," Mrs. McKittrick said.

That evening, after dinner, things began to seem more normal, again. Janet and Susanna arrived, then Vince and Buzzy rang the doorbell.

"Guess who's here?" said Mrs. McKittrick to the boys. "A surprise!"

There was an odd little silence. Then Vince said, "Well, for Pete's sake — Jack, too?"

"No, just Honey. She's only staying for a while. She came to visit. Let's all have a rum and cola and celebrate."

They went out on the lawn and sat beside the pool. At first the conversation seemed stilted, as if everyone, except perhaps Janet, were shyer in Honey's presence than before. Honey, too, seemed unsure of her new relationship to her old friends, and dropped into strange silences.

But the conversation picked up when they began to discuss the wedding.

"It was a great wedding," said Vince, "you should have seen old Buzz, after you left, Honey. He was so ravished by your perfidy he got stinko."

"Flu," said Buzzy.

"Tell me everything you did afterwards — What did you do, Vince?" Honey asked.

"We went out to the club. We didn't get home until dawn. It was a great old wedding."

"Terrific," Janet said.

Honey listened eagerly, almost wistfully, as if the role she had played in the wedding had been a minor and unfortunate one, preventing her from joining in the fun.

36

THE NEXT MORNING Janet called Buzzy and asked him to meet her after work at Miss Henderson's apartment. "It will be private, Henny won't be there, I have to talk to you."

When Buzzy arrived, Janet had the sherry bottle and glasses on the coffee table.

"Sit down and have a glass of something," she said.

Buzzy sat down on the sofa. He was dressed in blue jeans and a blue work shirt and was covered from head to foot with a fine dust from the mill. Janet began to pour the sherry.

"Thanks, none for me," said Buzzy.

"Oh, come on."

"No, thanks."

Janet poured herself a glass, and lit a cigarette. She took a long, thoughtful drag. "Well, I may as well begin," she said. "I'm sure you can guess the subject of the discussion."

"You're too mysterious for me," said Buzzy.

"Don't be silly. It's Honey, of course."

"What about Honey?" said Buzzy, in the same suddenly serious tone which Dr. McKittrick had used with Mrs. McKittrick, long ago, after Father Gerhardt had called.

"Well, what do you think?" said Janet. "I wanted your opinion, frankly."

"What do I think about what?"

"About what's happening."

"I'm not sure I dig you. What *is* happening?" Buzzy said.

Janet gave him a long, patient look. "Surely, you don't think it's *normal* for her to arrive home like this with absolutely no notice and no plans?"

"I don't know. I hadn't thought about it. Why shouldn't she?" Buzzy said.

"Think."

Buzzy grinned. "That's not my specialty," he said.

"Perhaps I made a mistake," Janet said. "I didn't mean to open up old wounds. I'm terribly sorry, Buzzy."

"Yeah, well you should be, Janet," Buzzy said. "There's nothing worse than an old wound-opener-up, but now, if you'll excuse me, I have to get home and take a shower."

"Perhaps you're not as — as sensitive as I thought?"

"Actually, I'm pretty insensitive," said Buzzy, cheerfully.

37

"THE WINDOW OF WOODWARD'S PHARMACY," Susanna read to Bennet. "Blank verse."

> *Rows of hot-water bottles hanging on hooks*
> *Alarm clocks*
> *Aspirin bottles piled in pyramids*
> *Syringes*
> *Pocket knives*
> *Coty's pale orange powder boxes with black*
>   *fleur-de-lis scattered upon them.*
>
> *Bathing caps*
> *Rubber water toys*
>
> *Displayed, though it is summer, on a winter*
>   *wonderland of fly-specked white cotton,*
>   *sprinkled with silvery foil.*

"Excellent," said Bennet.

"What about the divine inspiration?" Susanna said.

"That," said Bennet, "is between you and your Creator. We can only accept what we are given. Now, tell me about Honey." His voice sounded agitated.

Susanna told him.

"It is dramatically unacceptable," Bennet said. "Nothing can come of it. It encourages Mrs. McKittrick's weaknesses and makes Dr. McKittrick more sorrowful. It is needlessly hard for Buzzy Heffelfinger; it creates moral confusion and hinders the natural individual development of the other members of the Trio. But perhaps it is only a temporary aberration, and she will see the light."

38

A WEEK PASSED and Honey still lingered on. Sometimes Jack Parsons would call long distance, and Honey would take the phone into the coat closet and talk to him. When she came out Mrs. McKittrick would say, "How is Jack?" and Honey would say, "He's fine. He said to say 'hello' to everyone."

During the day she slept late, and then she would sunbathe or read magazines. Sometimes, for no apparent reason, she would burst into tears, or she and her mother would quarrel bitterly over some triviality, such as the use of separate butter plates on the table, or whether or not to change the beds.

"After all," Honey would say at such times, "I'm not a child. I'm a married woman."

On Saturday she had lunch with Susanna and Janet at the club.

"Well," said Janet, lifting her old-fashioned glass, "here's to the Trio. Now, tell us about married life."

"It's dreamy," said Honey.

"Details, please," said Janet. "Remember, we're the Trio."

"I meant, it's like a dream. All hazy. There aren't any details," Honey said.

39

ONE MORNING, Jack Parsons called Dr. McKittrick at his office. He had not yet settled on anything to call Dr. McKittrick — Dr. McKittrick being too formal — Bill, somehow, owing to their short acquaintance, seemed awkward. So he simply said, "This is Jack Parsons, your son-in-law."

"Why, hello, Jack, how are you?" said Dr. McKittrick, also feeling somewhat strained.

"I thought I'd just call up and see how everything was," said Jack. "Is Honey — all right?"

"Why, she's fine. It's nice to see her," Dr. McKittrick said. "How are things with you, Jack?"

"Fine. Well, I just wondered. Probably it would be better if you didn't mention I called."

"Of course," said Dr. McKittrick. "Nice of you to have inquired, though."

"Good-bye," said Jack.

"Good-bye," said Dr. McKittrick, realizing too late what an unsatisfactory conversation it had been.

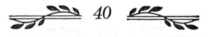

40

THE COUNTRY CLUB SUMMER BALL was on August 21st. Susanna was going with Buzzy, who had told Susanna that Vince was going to invite Janet. Nathan Brenner was also coming home on a three-day pass, and it would be necessary to find him a date.

"What about Honey?" said Janet to Susanna.

"What about her?"

"Well, we can't just let her sit home, can we?"

"But she's a married woman," said Susanna.

"That doesn't mean she has to be an old maid. Why doesn't Vince ask her?"

"But Vince is going to ask you."

"I know he'd rather take Honey," said Janet, stubbornly. "I'm going to suggest it to him. I can go with old Nathan, he won't mind."

"Oh, dear," said Honey, "I didn't bring a formal, but I guess I could ask Jack to send one up."

When Dr. McKittrick heard of this plan, he put his foot down for the first time. He said that Honey could stay with them as long as she liked, but that she was not going out with other men.

"But, Daddy, how can you call Vince another man?" Honey said.

"I can, because he is," said Dr. McKittrick, flatly.

So Buzzy took Susanna, and Nathan took Janet, and Vince went stag, and Honey stayed home. The night of the dance she wandered restlessly about. She put some records on the phonograph, then forgot to listen; she opened a book, and put it down. Then, impulsively, she walked out the door, across the lawn, and rang the Tidewater's bell.

Bennet was sitting in the living room with Mrs.

Tidewater, reading to her from *Pride and Preju-dice*. He received Honey graciously, and invited her to sit down.

"I shall be with you as soon as I finish this chap-ter," he said. "We're just coming to a very exciting part."

As he read, Mrs. Tidewater sat, her tiny body erect, her eyes fastened on Bennet's face. She did not look at Honey.

Good gracious! Lord bless me! [Bennet read] *Only think! Dear me! Mr. Darcy! Who would have thought it? And is it really true? Oh, my sweetest Lizzy! How rich and how great you will be! What pin-money, what jewels, what carriages you will have!*

Bennet stopped for a moment. "You remember Elizabeth didn't really care for material wealth, Mother?"

"I know she didn't, but I'm glad she has it, any-way," Mrs. Tidewater said.

Bennet read on, while Honey fidgeted, impa-tiently. At last, he closed the book.

"And now, if you will please excuse us, Mother, I am going to invite Honey up to my room."

Mrs. Tidewater gave a little sniff of consent.

"We'll finish the last chapter tomorrow evening," Bennet promised her.

They went to his room. Bennet gestured her toward one of the floor cushions, but she remained standing. Then he put the kettle on for tea. She knew that Bennet liked to follow his own rituals; in this case, it was evident he wished to make the tea before they talked. But she was too distraught to wait.

"I want to ask you something terribly personal," she said, bluntly.

Bennet went on about the preparations without responding.

"Have you noticed anything different about me?" Honey said.

The kettle whistled; Bennet poured the hot water into the heated silver pot; then, after waiting the proper length of time, he poured the tea.

Once more he gestured toward the cushion; Honey sat down. He presented her with a cup, then sat down, opposite her, with his own. Only after he had taken a sip, did he look at her, and say "Different?"

"The way I look."

"If anything, marriage has enhanced your physical charms."

"Then, if it isn't me, it must be everybody else. I

get so bored, just cooking for Jack, and then sitting around while he's at sea — sometimes for days at a time. The other wives all get together, then, and play bridge, but I never could concentrate on bridge, it was all such a bore. And if you even look at another man at a party, everyone thinks you're trying to seduce him. I came back for a little visit, just to have some fun. I thought it would be nice to see Norton and the Trio and all the boys again. But something's wrong. Everybody acts like I've got a disease or something. I mean, I know I'm married, and all, but I haven't changed that much, have I?" As if she were not quite certain, she rose and went to Bennet's mirror and studied her face. "Maybe I have," she said. "If you look carefully, there are some little lines around my mouth —"

"Why don't you call up Jack and tell him to come and get you?" Bennet said.

"Do you think I should?"

"I see no alternative, since you have made your wedding vows."

"You're as bad as everyone else," complained Honey.

"You knew what my position would be," said Bennet. "Isn't that why you came?"

"I suppose so."

"You are no longer the belle of Norton. You are a wife."

Honey gave a little shudder; then she sighed.

"Remember my warning, though. Beware of Janet. Don't go to her for advice."

Honey giggled. "Heavens, what could poor old Janet advise me about?" she said. "She can't even catch a man for herself."

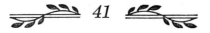

41

So JACK PARSONS came to reclaim his bride. He drove into town, but before he went to the McKittricks, he stopped at a service station and telephoned Janet.

"I just have a moment," he said, "but I thought I'd like to see you, first, if you don't mind."

They met downtown in Miss Henderson's apartment. Janet looked different to Jack. She seemed older, her clothes were more sophisticated, she had almost a maternal air.

"I keep a bottle at Henny's," she said to him. "Would you care for a drink?"

"Thank you, a short one. You can probably guess why I'm here."

Janet nodded, without changing her expression.

"The thing is, I don't seem to have — well — married anyone. No, I don't mean that. I mean, there is a mystery, it's hard to explain, a part of Honey I can't reach."

Janet lit a cigarette, and drew on it, slowly.

"I thought you might have some suggestions."

Janet sighed. "Oh, dear," she said, "it's just as I said, Honey is really basically insecure, deep down. And now that she doesn't have the Trio to hold her together, she's lost."

"I thought I might take the place of the Trio," Jack said.

"I wish I could say that would be easy," Janet said.

"What can I do?"

"We must all try to help her. By all, I mean you and me. I doubt if we can count on Susanna these days. If you don't mind my asking, how is her sexual adjustment?"

Jack Parsons blushed. "Why, all right, I guess," he said. "Why?"

"That's usually a problem in cases like this."

"It's funny, I hardly know you, but I feel I can really talk to you," Jack Parsons said. He glanced at his watch. "I suppose I had better go now, but I'm very grateful."

"Keep me informed," said Janet.

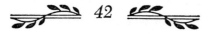 42

"TELL US ABOUT JACK PARSONS," one of Susanna's students asked, many years later.

"Bring me Volume I, please." Susanna opened the notebook. *"Jack Parsons,"* she said, *"was a splendid young man, who was killed in action early in the War at Guadalcanal."*

"That's *all* about Honey's husband?"

"Unfortunately, none of us could remember much. Honey, least of all. Bennet Tidewater, who was rejected by all branches of the service for reasons of health, tried to make Honey remember. He insisted that she write a physical description of her dead husband without looking at a photograph. This is what Honey wrote:

Blue eyes, well, blue-gray, maybe; straight nose, freckles; nice chin, sandy hair, good physique, very handsome, very dreamy.

Bennet said if he were grading the paper, she would receive a D—."

"What happened to Honey after Jack was killed?"

"After a brief period of mourning, she became a merry widow. An army camp was built near Norton, and she went to dances there every night, almost, for the duration. That is where she met Joseph Porter. They settled in Norton after the War. Joseph went into the lumber business, and became a rich man."

"And that is *all* about Jack Parsons?"

"That is all."

 *43*

"I THINK you can try people now," said Bennet to Susanna. "Describe Mrs. McKittrick carrying trays of food to the pool."

Susanna shut her eyes. "She makes funny little clumping steps. Her heels are too high, and they sink down in the grass. The tray is awkward. Arthur follows her. She talks to Arthur on the way. She tells him the food isn't for him, it's for company. She says she is sorry, but perhaps there will be a tiny tidbit left over, if he is a good dog. No one, watching her, is certain she will reach her destination without a disaster; there is a feeling of tension in the air."

"Describe Dr. McKittrick going to bed."

"He stands up and yawns and stretches dramatically. Then he says, 'Well, it's time for my beauty sleep. See you in the spring.'"

"Describe Buzzy Heffelfinger."

"Loose-jointed, sappy, sandy all over, with freckled skin. Sparkling blue eyes shine out of his face like a blue oasis in a desert."

"Hmmm," said Bennet.

"Yes?" said Susanna.

"Continue, please."

"An excellent dancer and tennis player. Natural leadership qualities, which he executes in a quiet, unassuming way. He is lighthearted and loyal, and above all, tough."

"Is he as tough as Janet?"

"Tougher."

"Is he as tough as Honey?"

"They are equally tough."

"Describe Janet."

"Janet? Oh, dear, I couldn't!"

"For heaven's sakes, why not?"

"Well, I guess I know her too well. After all, she's a member of the Trio!"

"You still have a ways to go," Bennet said.

44

"Now THAT TURKY'S GONE, and I hope you don't think it's sacrilegious if I say, 'Good riddance,' I've been thinking very seriously about my leaving this stifling atmosphere, which by the way, Turky made more poisonous, and taking an apartment in San Francisco," said Henny to Janet.

"Norton is not the world."

"You can say that again. When I was gone, recently, on my little trip, I said to Mr. Masters — by the way, did I mention that he is stationed down there? — that I felt I could breathe for the first time in years. Actually *breathe*. Isn't that fantastic? I could sit at a cabaret bar in the old Barbary Coast area, and sip a martini cocktail, and take in the atmosphere, without feeling there was someone watching me from behind every post. And I thought of you, Janet. To be brutally frank, I don't think you're appreciated here, either."

"They want me to stay on at Hinks," said Janet. "They have raised my salary."

"Hinks! Of course, if you really want to spend

your life selling carpets and curtains to the bour-
geoisie —"

"The funny thing is, I'm good at it," Janet said
regretfully. "I used to envy Honey so, for having
such an interesting house. Perhaps that's why."

"Then you are still bound to the Trio," said
Henny, sadly.

"Do you think I could find a job in San Francisco?"

"Mr. Masters says jobs are plentiful now for
women. They are even driving cabs."

"Perhaps I could work up to be a buyer."

"If you can escape from Norton, dear."

"Of course I can. Why shouldn't I?"

"I don't know. It's just a wee feeling I have, a
funny little feeling that you won't be able to *quite*
make the break."

"You don't think I'm strong enough?" said Janet.
Henny smiled.

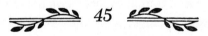 45

IT WAS LATE SEPTEMBER. The pears were picked,
and shipped, the transient workers gone. A crisp

smell of fall was in the air. School had begun, and with it, football weather.

Susanna had stayed with the *News Sentinel*. With Honey and Janet both gone, the Pi Phi House, for her, would have been empty. The newspaper, she decided, would give her the practical experience she needed.

In Locals and Personals, she wrote:

Mr. Richard, "Buzzy," Heffelfinger and Mr. Vincent Holbrook, Norton High School graduates and students at the University of Oregon, have departed for Camp Pendleton, California, where they will be training as United States Marines.

Dr. and Mrs. William McKittrick are visiting their daughter and son-in-law, Ensign and Mrs. John Parsons, in San Diego. Mrs. Parsons's wedding was a highlight of the Winter social season.

Mrs. Bennet Tidewater, and her son, Bennet, are leaving this week to reside in Los Angeles for the duration of the War, where Bennet Tidewater will be employed in defense work in an aircraft factory.

Miss Janet Springer, employee of Hinks Department Store, has recently been promoted to Buyer in Interior Decoration.

Two weeks later, Susanna wrote:

Miss Janet Springer has recently resigned from her position as Buyer in Interior Decoration at Hinks Department Store to reside in San Francisco. She will share an apartment with Miss Louise Henderson, formerly an English teacher at Norton High School.

 *46*

ONE DAY WHEN SUSANNA came home from work she found a letter addressed to her upon the hall table. The outside was marked "Personal." Because it was marked this way, Roger had steamed it open; finding neither money nor anything of interest to him — it was just from Janet Springer — he had sealed it up again.

Dear Susanna [wrote Janet],

Well, Norton is not the world, and I guess I have found this out maybe the hard way, but still I have no regrets. Henny and I have had a falling out. I could no longer put up with her sitting around the apartment all day doing nothing but drink. I actually began to sympathize with Miss Turknet, of all people. It seems that there are always two sides to a story!

To be brief, I was forced to ask her to depart, and I am now alone. Well, I have my job at the Emporium, which is more than Henny ever had, and I am now formally inviting you to join me.

Susanna, when I said Norton is not the world, I thought of you becoming a writer. How can you become one if you stay in that hick town and never broaden your perspectives? Remember Dickens and Shakespeare — San Francisco could be your London. What's there to write about in Norton? Henny was correct about that. To be brutally frank, Susanna dear, I don't think you're appreciated there.

If you come, we'll go to operas and the theatre and museums and simply swill down culture. There are divine men in uniform all over the streets. I have painted one wall lime green and the other oyster.

Have you heard from Honey? What's new at the McKittricks? Please, please bring all *the latest gossip.*

You have to come, we're all that's left of the Trio, it is your Duty."

Lots of love,

Janet

P.S.: Don't tell anyone about Henny, and this means Bennet Tidewater, too.

Susanna, who missed Bennet Tidewater, and also Buzzy and Vince and Teddy and Nathan, came.

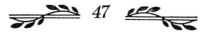

47

"Janet didn't ask henny to leave, did she?" said Barby Hall to Susanna at teatime.

"That is correct. Henny simply vanished one day. She left no note, nor did she pay her share of the rent. She followed Mr. Masters to Seattle, where he had been transferred."

"Why didn't Janet tell you the truth; after all, you were the Trio?" said Bitsy.

"She was hurt by Henny's desertion, wasn't she?" said Cathy.

"Yes, she was hurt, and she possessed a terrible pride," Susanna said.

48

"THERE IS NO ONE AROUND, everyone has gone," said Mrs. McKittrick to Dr. McKittrick. "There is no one to look at our Tree, why do I even bother to have one, I wonder?"

"Well, it wouldn't be Christmas without a Tree," said the Doctor. "Look, Arthur likes it. He's wagging his tail."

"Arthur is getting too fat," Mrs. McKittrick said. "Please don't throw the tinsel on that way. I'll just have to take it off and do it all over. Arthur is useless. All he cares about is getting fed. Let's put him to sleep."

"You're hurting Arthur's feelings."

"Arthur has no feelings," Mrs. McKittrick said.

 *49*

DURING THE REST OF THE WAR, Susanna lived with Janet in San Francisco, and taught on emergency credentials in a public high school. Janet was acquiring a circle of new friends, but Susanna spent her weekends writing stories, using San Francisco, usually, as a locale. She sent these out to magazines; ordinarily, she received a printed rejection slip, but, occasionally, she was sent a personal note from an editor.

Dear Miss Swope,

San Francisco is certainly a very picturesque setting, and I envy you living there. But, somehow, we do not feel you have quite caught its flavor. The high school prom you have described sounds rather old-fashioned and small-townish, and the heroine, though pretty, seems rather dull. But do try us again.

Dear Miss Swope,

Your short story, "After the Wedding," has a certain poignancy, especially when the young naval officer was killed. But we were all shocked at the behavior of the widow, afterwards. Were you trying to be funny or sad? At such a time we do not feel it would benefit our readers or our country to publish it.

Dear Miss Swope,

The three young ladies in your story, "The Trio," just don't seem to have what it takes, I'm afraid. They seem terribly uninteresting. Why three girls, of nubile age, would spend their days drinking tea and being preached at by such a dreary, sexless young man is beyond me, and I'm afraid would be beyond our readers. I say this regretfully, because your scenes of San Francisco are fun.

Dear Miss Swope,

Your description of the New Guinea jungles was nicely done, but your missionary hero, who is eaten by the natives, is a bit much. Perhaps you should try a church publication.

Susanna treasured these notes; she filed them neatly away, until the day came when she left Janet's apartment to assume her new position at Miss Parker's School for Girls. Then she cleaned out her files and burned the rejection slips.

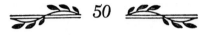 *50*

"Tell us about the war," said Cathy to Susanna at teatime.

"Yes, tell us what happened to everyone," Barby said.

"Bring me my War Journal, please," said Susanna. This was a special notebook, entitled *The War and After,* in which she had inscribed the fates of both active participants and civilians. She had begun with the Dead, not because, as she told the girls, the worst thing was being killed, but because it was a convenient beginning.

The War and After

1. Jack Parsons, killed Guadalcanal — 1942.

2. Teddy Lyons, killed — Normandy landing, D-Day.

3. Buzzy Heffelfinger, blinded by Japanese shell on Iwo Jima. Trained by government to use Seeing Eye Dog. Returned to college, studied law.

(*See* "*Clippings*" — Reader's Digest, *Jan.,
1947, "A Blind Veteran's New Buddy.*")

After practicing law in Norton (*See* "*Clippings*" — Sat. Eve. Post, *April 1951, "Heffelfinger
and Browner — Oregon's Novel Law Partner-
ship*"), *he ran for State Legislature, 1956. Won.*

Ran for U. S. Congress, won, 1960. (*See Clippings,*" Life *Magazine, June 1, 1961, "The Special
Vision of Oregon's New Blind Congressman.*")

*4. Vince Holbrook, Marine Corps, saw action in
South Pacific. After war, returned to college, studied medicine. Joined Dr. McKittrick's practice.
After Dr. McKittrick's death, became Norton's
leading physician. Married to Stella Marsh, who
was a New Girl. Looked after Mrs. McKittrick's
health, visited her frequently, until she accused
Stella of trying to steal her Imari bowl, and ordered
them both from her house forever.*

*5. Nathan Brenner became a professor of Eco-
nomics, University of California. Married one of
his students. Four children.*

*6. Bennet Tidewater, rejected by all branches of
service. Moved with mother to Los Angeles, worked
in aircraft factory for duration. Murdered shortly
after war in misunderstanding in bar.*

*7. Dr. McKittrick considered joining service as
physician, but Mrs. McKittrick began her Nervous
Breakdown at this time, and he was prevented*

from carrying out this plan. Died, heart attack, 1960.

8. Mr. Springer committed suicide on top of Little Butte with antique Colt revolver, which had once belonged to pioneer Hawley family.

9. Mrs. Springer, died, cancer, 1950.

10. Roger Swope, too young to enter service, became criminal. Apprehended, June, 1946, robbing filling station. Served two years, State Penitentiary. Now successful real estate man in Portland. Wife, three children.

11. Dr. Swope, died, complications from diabetes, 1959.

12. Mrs. Swope, sold home when husband died, moved to Hilltop Senior Citizens Home, where she is, at present, Social Co-ordinator.

13. Harry Nakamura, Japanese Relocation Center, Tule Lake, 1941–42. Released to serve in armed forces in Italy. Returned to college after war, became orthodontist in Norton. Also President of Junior Chamber of Commerce.

14. Miss Maribell Turknet joined WAC's, remained in them after war.

15. Miss Louise Henderson became Camp Follower. When Mr. Masters was sent overseas, she took up with other army men. When last heard of was in sanitorium for alcoholics in Arizona.

16. Honey, after period of mourning, became

merry widow. Married Joseph Porter in 1948. Has two daughters, named after Janet and me.

17. Janet pursued career in San Francisco. Became Interior Decorator, A.I.D. Became very chic. In 1956, married Gerald Kroner, a Mystery Person. (See Volume II, Gerald Kroner.)

18. Susanna Swope joined Janet Springer in San Francisco. Shared apartment with her for a year and taught on emergency credentials in public schools. At end of this year took position teaching in Miss Parker's School for Girls in Mill Valley. Has led simple, but exemplary life.

"Congressman Heffelfinger has never married, has he?" said Barby.

"His heart belongs to Honey," Bitsy said.

Susanna looked at her severely. "I am not certain I have ever quite said that," she said.

"Oh, I know it does. For one thing, being blinded, he remembers her in all her youthful splendor."

"Naturally, that is how he remembers her, being blinded. But where his heart belongs at the moment, I could not say. How can one tell what goes on inside hearts? A girl I had several years ago was absolutely positive that Joseph Porter would marry Janet. This did not occur. We must try to be faithful to facts. By the way, what is a fact?"

"Facts are truth," said Cathy.

"I am not sure that they are," said Susanna, "but it is all that we have. At least, it is all that I have, and I try to limit myself to them. Bennet Tidewater considered them a necessary discipline and hoped someday I would get beyond them, but I am not sure what he meant. It is quite possible I have a stunted nature; I have considered this. Perhaps you, Bitsy, can see things I cannot see, in which case we should be glad to have you instruct us. However, there is not time, now, there is the bell."

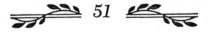 *51*

"I'M NOT SURE I ever told you about the Emerson Grade School," Janet said, one Sunday afternoon to Gerald Kroner. They had been married two weeks, and were living in Janet's apartment; they were going to move to a marvelous old huge shingled "cottage" in Sausalito, which Gerald had picked out, as soon as he got an expected textile contract from a new hotel that was being built in the city. He had no office, but worked out of the apartment while Janet was gone. Swatches of materials and sample books were draped about in an untidy way; he ate lunch out in some elegant restaurant with a contractor or executive for the hotel; she was not certain how he spent the rest of his time; he was not up when she left in the morning.

"If it has anything to do with Sugar —" said Gerald. He lay stretched out upon Janet's white sofa, staring moodily out at the Bay. He was rather moody, she had discovered. He was dressed in his Sunday clothes, black corduroy trousers which had a sheen like velvet, a white knit polo shirt and a black golf cardigan with puff sleeves; on his feet he wore black Italian loafers.

"You mean Honey," she said.

"Sugar, Honey, Sweetie. Whatever. Or Bennet What's-His-Name. If it's about them, then you have undoubtedly told me." His voice was sleepy, and rather English at the same time. In an odd way he reminded her of her father, though he lacked her father's quaint, gentlemanly manners.

"The Honey Bunch," said Gerald.

"The what?" said Janet, her voice rising.

"Isn't that what you called yourselves?"

"We called ourselves the Trio. Everyone called us that."

"The Honey Bunch would have been better," said Gerald, lazily.

She was about to reply that he knew nothing about it, could not possibly know; that, moreover, she resented his assumption that he could. Instead, she forced herself to be humble. "I wasn't going to talk about that," she said. "It was something else. Would you like me to make you some tea?"

"You're always wanting to make me something. I'm extremely comfortable."

She smiled, and sat down opposite him. "It was just that, you see, I went to the Emerson Grade School, which was built on the land my father used to own."

"Edwin Springer, Realtor. Too bad he didn't know how to hang on to his own real estate."

"He never thought of it as real estate, it was our orchard."

"That was undoubtedly his mistake."

"Undoubtedly. But it *was* a funny feeling — I felt like one of those misunderstood heroines who ran an inn in what was once their ancestral home."

"Did you always think of yourself as a heroine?" said Gerald.

"I was a romantic child. I fed on — on fantasy."

"It seems to me you still do," said Gerald Kroner. He rose slowly, and picked up a magazine from the coffee table. Then he resettled himself and began to leaf through it. After a few moments he said, "What did your Dr. Kedy have to say about that?"

"About — ?" said Janet.

"Feeding on fantasy."

"It was something — to be overcome."

"Well, why don't we start? Today."

"I didn't mean to bore you. I just think of things I'd like to tell you. Sometimes I feel you don't really know me, you've only seen me in my present environment. I guess I'd like you to tell me things, too — about *your* childhood."

"My childhood is over," said Gerald Kroner. "I see nothing to gain by discussing it. You can discuss yours with Dr. Kedy."

"It's only that, it's hard to explain, I'd just like to talk. For fun."

"What I was going to suggest is that you stop your subscription to that newspaper. The Norton Gazette."

"The *News Sentinel?*"

"That would be a step forward, I believe."

"No," said Janet, "I won't." Her tone of voice surprised her; there were sudden tears in her eyes.

"It was only a suggestion," said Gerald Kroner.

52

SUSANNA VISITED HER MOTHER four times a year after her father's death. Roger, who had become an exemplary citizen, filled in between times. Mrs. Swope was not unhappy; at the Hilltop Senior Citizens Home, she was, at various times, chairman of the program committee, of the recreation tours, and co-ordinator of social activities. This left Susanna free to visit Honey, as well as other old friends. One day she called upon Mrs. Tidewater, who had moved back to Norton after Bennet's death.

Mrs. Tidewater could not afford the Hilltop; she lived in a small stucco duplex on the wrong side of town, near the Emerson School. She received Susanna, warily.

"I am a very old woman," she told Susanna, as she let her in. Though she had always been small, she had shrunk even more. Her brown mousy hair, now white, was sparse; her skull shone through the bald spots. She was wearing an old brown dress and bedroom slippers. She invited Susanna to sit down on a chair, and she sat down, with difficulty, opposite her. There were only two familiar objects in the room: the German piano, with the photographs of Bennet upon it, and Bennet's silver tea set, on a table.

I can't just ask what happened, though that is what I have come for, Susanna thought. She said, "I have been wanting to pay my respects for a long time."

"I'm not used to visitors," Mrs. Tidewater said. "But somebody did come the other day. That man who is married to Honey. He wanted to know if there was anything he could do for me. What could he do? Why did he come? I have a small pension, which is adequate for my needs."

"I suppose he was just being thoughtful," Susanna said.

"He didn't know Bennet. He had no business coming here," Mrs. Tidewater said, proudly.

"You have had a great tragedy," said Susanna, "and there is nothing anyone can say."

"Nothing whatsoever," Mrs. Tidewater agreed.

"Perhaps the memory of his religious nature helps you."

"If there is a God," said Mrs. Tidewater, "He had no right to take Bennet from me. For that matter, I sometimes think Bennet was ungrateful to die."

"We know very little about his death," Susanna said. "Would it help you to talk about it?"

"He was shot dead in a bar by a madman," Mrs. Tidewater said. "He was not the sort of person who went to places like that. No one can tell me why he was there. He usually spent his evenings at home with me. Perhaps there was more of his father in him than I care to think."

"He served tea to me so often, from that lovely pot," Susanna said.

Mrs. Tidewater seemed confused.

"The tea set, on the table, over there," said Susanna.

"Oh, that," said Mrs. Tidewater. "He collected things. They mean nothing to me, anymore — nothing at all." She looked at Susanna sharply. "Would you like to have it?" she said.

"Oh, I wouldn't dream of taking it from you," Susanna said.

"You were a member of that Trio," said Mrs. Tidewater, in a dead tone. "You and Honey and that other one. You were the only friends he ever seemed to care for. I don't know why, but it doesn't matter. You may take the tea set."

"Well, that's really terribly sweet of you," said Susanna.

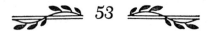

53

WHEN JOSEPH PORTER first saw Janet's apartment, he gave a long low whistle of admiration. "Honey told me you had taste," he said.

Janet, who did not care for the word "taste," and who was also busy observing Joseph for the first time, did not reply to the compliment. Instead she said, "I'm disappointed that Honey didn't come."

"Me, too. Hell, I've tried to talk her into a trip for years. I said, 'Come on down for the lumber convention, it'll be good for you.' "

"What did she say?" said Janet.

She had not yet invited Joseph to sit down. He stood in her living room, a large, stocky man, wearing a hard finish dark gray suit with padding in the shoulders, a tie with a horrid runny pattern, a jeweled tie clip, matching cuff links and winged-tip shoes. He had a new haircut, which gave him a skinned appearance. But his eyes were large and brown and kindly; his voice was deep and pleasant. When he had shaken hands with her, he had gripped her hand warmly, as if he were meeting a long lost friend.

"Oh, you know, the girls," said Joseph. "There's always something, I guess. Your namesake had a piano recital this time."

Janet lit a cigarette, and gestured to Joseph to sit down. But he remained awkwardly standing, until she sat down.

"We can have drinks, here, and then go out for dinner, if that's what you'd like," she said, tentatively. Where could she take him, she wondered. She felt he might feel ill at ease in one of her favorite intimate French restaurants, that he might be somehow disappointed in a typical San Francisco one, like Jack's, or Sam's.

"Listen, I promised Honey we'd do the town. That's some view you have. I wish she could see it. She wants me to bring back all the news. She apologizes for never writing. And I'm supposed to say —" he hesitated slightly, "that she's sorry about the divorce."

"Oh, that," said Janet, "is Ancient History. It was a very short-lived marriage, you know."

"It happens all over. Norton, too. You don't have to explain."

"I won't." She smiled at Joseph. "Bourbon? Scotch? Martini?"

"I'll make 'em," he said. "That's what a man's for."

"So," he said, over dinner at Julius Castle, "I've finally met the Missing Link."

"You mean — the 'Trio?' " she laughed.

"What else? I've felt a little left out, you know. The Stranger in Town. I've only lived there twelve years. But I didn't know the Trio in its heyday."

"We were rather famous, I suppose."

"Don't tell me," he begged, humorously. He leaned across the table toward her. "Too bad Bennet Tidewater isn't alive," he said.

Janet looked startled.

"I mean, that would be the whole picture, wouldn't it?"

"You sound as if we're a jigsaw puzzle."

"You are," he said, earnestly.

"Then Honey talks to you — about us?"

"Sometimes. Sometimes her mother. Sometimes Buzzy Heffelfinger. Sometimes Vince. Sometimes just people I meet on the street. You left your mark, you three." He did not sound happy.

"It's bothered you," she said with sudden sympathy.

"Now and then. It's hard to explain. It sounds silly. Honey has a way of looking — as if she's staring into the past."

"She tosses her head and a lock of hair falls over one eye —"

Now it was Joseph's turn to look astonished.

"It isn't easy being beautiful," said Janet.

"That's just it — I mean, she's my wife, she's beautiful to me, but, well, we're all getting on. We've been married ten years, now. By the way, I brought some snapshots." He produced his wallet. "This is Honey. It's an old photo, a few years ago — she won't let me take her picture, now. We were up at our cabin on the river. That's me, there with the fish."

Janet took the snapshot; it was not a good one; Honey's face was a blur. Her figure in blue jeans looked matronly. Was this the photograph, she wondered; or could Honey really have let her figure go like this? She felt dazed.

"This is Jan, your namesake, and this is Susie. Susie's going to be taller than Jan."

"They look like nice girls."

"Oh, Honey's a good mother. She devotes all her time to them. Too much for her own good, I think, sometimes. They're standing in front of our house — we built it three years ago."

Janet saw a new, postwar, expensive-looking ranch house, with a shake roof and board and batten exterior.

"It's very nice," she said.

"But this, here, is my prize possession, my plane. It's for business, but it takes me fishing, too. I named it after Honey, but she won't go up in it. She's nervous flying."

He put the pictures back in his wallet. There was an awkward silence. Janet could think of nothing to say. Then Joseph said, "When I mentioned we were all getting on, well, I guess you're the exception. I didn't expect, that is, I thought you'd look older. What I'm trying to say, I guess, is that it's funny —"

Janet lit a cigarette, nervously.

"What I'm getting at —" said Joseph.

"Is that Honey getting older doesn't seem to matter, she's still the Beauty of the Trio," Janet said.

"It doesn't make sense," said Joseph.

"But it's true, anyway," said Janet, quietly.

They went to the Top of the Mark, and then to North Beach. Janet had not visited these places for years; she was amazed at what a good time she was having, at how quickly the evening went by. She was surprised, too, that she enjoyed Joseph's appreciativeness.

"This is a great city, isn't it? Isn't it funny, how you and Susanna left and Honey stayed in Norton. You're a real City Girl, aren't you?"

"I should be, by now. I'm not sure, though. I think about Norton a lot."

"Are you sorry you left? Honey thinks you must be."

Janet laughed. "That's so like Honey. But I had to leave. It was right for me," she said.

At midnight they went back to her apartment. Janet poured two glasses of brandy, and handed one to Joseph.

"Well, here's to your meeting the Missing Link," she said.

He put the glass down and took her in his arms. Since Gerald, she had slept around, the vulgar term was really quite suitable; it had been a form of therapy, almost like taking sitting up exercises to recover from surgery. But when this rather awkward, gentle man touched her, she had to stifle a cry.

Later, he said, "Bennet Tidewater once told Honey that you would betray her."

She felt a strange chill. "Then I guess we couldn't help ourselves, could we?" she said in a bright little voice.

"Hell, I shouldn't have said that," Joseph said.

54

ON THE AFTERNOON of the Reunion Luncheon, Joseph paid a visit to his mother-in-law. He visited her regularly once a week. He had assumed this duty on his own; Honey had never asked him, nor even thanked him for it.

Honey almost never visited her mother, herself. As she told Joseph, visiting made no difference to the old lady; her mother did not welcome her when she came nor remember the visit after she left.

For a time, after his daughters were born, Joseph Porter would take them to visit, too; but, as they grew older this became more difficult. Mrs. McKittrick either insisted they were the children of that "dear, dead handsome boy," and commiserated with them on their fatherless state, or she would call them Janet and Susanna (instead of Jan and Susie), and talk to them as if they were members of that disgusting Trio. Joseph stopped taking them altogether when his mother-in-law asked Jan, the elder, if she thought Honey was still a virgin.

"You probably think I am narrow-minded, but I'm not," she said, when Joseph had protested. "I am young in spirit. People have always said so. I have an affinity with young people, if I do say so, myself!"

Mrs. McKittrick seldom left her house since the Doctor died five years ago. She had dropped all of her old friends. She had, however, inspired new loyalties. One was Mrs. Mavis Gage, the mother-in-law of Roger Swope, who did Mrs. McKittrick's hair once a week at the Fountain of Beauty. Another was the cabdriver, Fred Walters, who gallantly assisted her to his taxi, brought a lap rug on cold days, and did errands for her, while she was under the dryer. A third was a handyman, Bob Blair, who made necessary repairs at the house. There was also a woman who waited on tables at the Country Club; Honey knew her name.

Occasionally, when Joseph had dropped in to see his mother-in-law, he would find one of this group, sitting with Mrs. McKittrick drinking gin and tonic, or beer, and watching television. Though Joseph knew it was good for her to have company, he could not keep himself from being irritated. He was the intruder; the others were her cronies. Joseph was not a snob, but he was puzzled by this doctor's widow finding her new friends among the working class.

On important issues, Mavis would intercede for Joseph. She persuaded Mrs. McKittrick to permit Dr. Madison, who was Vince Holbrook's partner, to drop by twice a year to give her a checkup; to allow a furnaceman in to repair the furnace; to let a cousin of Mavis's come in once a month and clean out the refrigerator and vacuum. But, beyond these interventions for the sake of health and welfare, Mavis was loyal. No personal comments concerning her eccentric customer ever passed her lips.

For a time, Joseph had been concerned that Mrs. McKittrick was buying these friendships, was paying her "friends" more than their services deserved. But Mrs. McKittrick would complain about the high price of taxis, of hair sets, of yard work; one day she told Joseph she was upset; she had accidentally tipped Mavis more than ten percent. The loyalty this crazy old woman inspired was evidently not purchased; once extravagant, in her old age Mrs. McKittrick had turned miserly.

The Lower Hill was now zoned for nonresidential use. The Tidewater house had been replaced by a three-story office building; the Swope house was, quite appropriately, a dental clinic. In the midst of this commercial development, the Mc-

Kittrick home, surrounded by the iron fence Mrs. McKittrick had put up when the Doctor died, had the look of a fortified ruin. The lawn had gone to seed; the porch pillars leaned, the walls were textured with peeling paint. Since Bob Blair spent part of the day he worked here drinking and watching television with his employer, he could not keep up with the deterioration.

"Have you ever thought of going to the Hilltop Senior Citizens Home?" Joseph had asked his mother-in-law one day.

"When I leave this house," she told him, "it will be in my coffin."

Joseph unwound the wire which fastened the gate, and walked up the untended, weedy path to the front door. He rang the bell, a meaningless courtesy he always observed. Then he tried the door. It was locked, as usual. He took out the key, which he had had made, and entered the dark hall. The television was blaring in the den. His mother-in-law watched television all day and half the night.

He walked into the den; Mrs. McKittrick sat, straight and tiny, on a straight chair, in front of the set. She wore one of her queer costumes — this time a brown lace tea gown, from what Joseph imagined was the thirties or early forties. On her feet were high white satin slippers; her white hair was tightly coiffed; she looked oddly elegant, as if she were waiting to receive guests.

"Hello, Mother," Joseph shouted.

She glanced up at Joseph without curiosity, then turned back to the set.

"I'm watching 'What's My Line?'" she said in her strange flat voice.

"I just thought I'd drop in and see how you were getting along. The children are fine. So is Honey."

"Honey?"

"Your daughter, Honey."

"Yes, my daughter is very beautiful. It's a pity she never married after that sweet boy was killed. He was her life."

"Come, come, Mother. You know she's married to me." Joseph turned off the television, and pulled up a chair next to her.

"After 'What's My Line,' I watch Art Linkletter." she whined.

"That isn't very sociable. I've come to visit you. I have some news. Janet and Susanna are in town. They're having lunch with Honey at the Country Club today. It's a Reunion. If you like, they might drop in to see you."

"I don't see people. I wouldn't trust Susanna in the house. She's such a quiet, sneaky little thing. You never know when she's around. I think she steals. She stole the Doctor's decoy ducks from this very room."

"You sold those, Mother, when you did this room over."

"I did it in Pennsylvania Dutch. Hearts and flowers. But I don't decorate anymore. I don't need to. I have things just the way I like them. Everyone wants to get in and see what I've done, but I don't let them. My home is not a museum, no matter what they may think."

"Would you like to see Janet, Mother?"

"I would not. She's become a Decorator, you know, but she's not going to steal my ideas. Everyone always said I was original, and I am. I'm not afraid to express my Personality, like Janet. She's become hoity-toity. They brought that girl up like Russian nobility after the Revolution, the Doctor used to say."

"Tell me about the Trio," Joseph said.

"They were thick as thieves. Spoiled, sassy little girls. They made our house a regular club. Boys all over the place. But they came to see me, after Honey left. They liked me, too. I made them the most beautiful hors d'oeuvres, if I do say so, myself."

"Why don't you see them now, Mother? Why did you stop seeing people?"

"You can't party all of your life. My house is not

a clubhouse. When the Doctor died, I had the pool filled in. I planted an Elizabethan garden over it."

"Tell me about Bennet Tidewater, Mother."

"That sissy little fellow. His mother overprotected him. I don't know what the girls saw there. They wouldn't even take him in the service. He was some kind of religious nut. I've never believed in religions. I don't like the way ministers think they can just drop in on you, without any notice. I might be stark naked, you know. You don't need ministers, anyhow. They're just after your money. God is within you. That's my belief."

"Honey is a Catholic, now, Mother."

"It's an emotional thing. Sex, obviously. If she wants to sleep with any Tom, Dick or Harry, it's her business. I only slept with one man in all my life, and that was quite enough for me."

"Honey is married to me, Mother."

"That's what you think. I know her. I brought her up, didn't I? People gasped when she came down the aisle. All the boys were in love with her. That Congressman, what's his name?"

"Buzzy."

"Buzzy worshipped the ground she walked on. But the time wasn't right, not then. However, beauty isn't everything. Beauty is as beauty does, I always said. Would you like to see my table decoration? Mavis and Fred helped me with it. We worked all evening, then we had beer and watched the wrestling matches."

She led Joseph into the dining room. The curtains were pulled, as always. He switched on a light, and nothing happened. In the gloom, he saw the table, set formally for six guests. She had used a dark green cloth, and put out her best white china rimmed with gold; the napkins were gold-colored; the silver shone. The centerpiece looked to be part of an old Christmas decoration, consisting of tiny apples sprayed with gold paint. On the sideboard stood a dazzling silver tea set.

"Forest green and gold, the motif of Honey's wedding," she said. Then, coyly, "This dress is the one I wore. Do you think it's becoming? I want you to give me your honest answer."

"Extremely. But you look a little thin. Are you eating? Is Mr. Maddox delivering your groceries?"

"I won't have people coming into the house. The Doctor left me a wealthy woman, and everyone knows it."

"How do you get your groceries, Mother?"

"I have him leave them on the back porch."

"Mr. Maddox told me sometimes they've piled up there for days."

"It's time for Art Linkletter," she cried, in panic.

"All right, I'll leave. But be a good girl, and eat," Joseph said.

This was one of her bad days, he thought, as he walked back down the overgrown path. But why should this depress him so? What did he want from her? After all, she was just a pathetic old woman.

Mrs. McKittrick stood behind the curtain of the den, and watched Joseph leave. Why did this young man pester her so, she wondered. He was such a stupid young man. He had had no right to marry Honey. He hadn't even known her until after that nice young man was killed. He hadn't known the Doctor, or Teddy Lyons, or Bennet Tidewater. He had not known Buzzy until he was blinded. He had never visited their home when she had entertained for Honey's beaux; he had never seen the parties around the swimming pool; he had never seen Arthur. He had not known the Trio in its prime. And always questions, questions. "Tell me about Bennet Tidewater? Tell me about the Trio?" But no matter how many questions he asked, he never seemed to get any brighter. And he never would; it was hopeless.

Well, Honey will fix him, she thought. She had always managed things her way. She wished, though, she would hurry up, so this stupid young man who would never get any brighter, would leave her alone.

55

JANET HAD NOT BEEN IN NORTON since her mother had died fifteen years ago. All during those years she had seen the town in her mind, it had appeared in her dreams, it was the setting for her stream of consciousness musings on Dr. Kedy's couch; as she grew older it had begun to figure in anecdotes which she told her friends.

"I can't explain it, you'd have to live there," she would say, evoking a special, quaint, even aristocratic background for her girlhood.

"All ages knew one another. The pace was different, too. No one seemed in a hurry. We had time."

Had her mind been playing tricks on her; or was the town playing tricks on her, now? Its very familiarity made it seem more foreign to her than a town she had never seen before. Discounting the expected changes — old buildings torn down, new buildings put up, Main Street changed to a one-way thoroughfare, this sort of thing — the town was just as she remembered it, but not quite.

But this not-quiteness made all the difference. It was like one of those picture-games in newspapers where you are supposed to guess "What Is Wrong with This Picture?" What *was* wrong? Something must be, or she would not be experiencing this odd uneasiness. Yes, the town was playing tricks on her. She might have known, it had never really been friendly, it was laughing at her behind her back.

Oh, really, she thought, I'm not *that* — paranoid. I know towns don't play tricks on people. Dr. Kedy has seen real progress. I must not slip, now.

But why then did everything here on Main Street seem just slightly out of kilter, as if she were seeing it in a mirror turned around? There was the library, across from the Jackson Hotel, where she and Susanna were staying. (And how odd it was to stay in a hotel in the town where you had grown up!) There was the library, a Greek temple, surrounded by plane trees. If she walked up the steps, between the two stone ladies— she even remembered their names, Truth and Beauty — and walked inside, she would know just how it would smell. Why then did it seem unreal? She stood on the sidewalk in front of the hotel and stared at it. Passersby must think she was crazy. Well, maybe she was. What was the matter with the library?

She walked on down the street toward the heart

of town. She had two hours while Susanna was visiting her mother. (Susanna thought she had business to attend to.) It was very warm. She passed
men in their shirt sleeves and women in sleeveless
cotton dresses. She, herself, was dressed in a dark
cotton suit from I. Magnin's, and black patent
leather pumps. She looked, obviously, like a stranger. What did they think? But the funny thing was
no one looked at her. Was *she* real? Did *she* exist?
No one seemed to notice her at all.

Look at me, she wanted to say. Look! I am a native, I was born here. My father was Edwin
Springer, we used to own the Springer Orchard,
where the Emerson School is now. My father
wrote (but did not finish) *The History of Norton
County,* and shot himself on top of Little Butte.
My mother founded the local Stratford Club. I was
a member of the famous Trio. I am having — no, I
had an affair with Joseph Porter, Honey McKittrick's second husband. How much more can you
belong to a place than this? But she was like Rip
Van Winkle without even a dog to recognize her.

Well, she could always drop in on people. She
could see Vince or Buzzy if he were home from
Washington, or even Harry Nakamura. She still
knew some of the merchants, who would remember
her parents. She could always go up to the second
floor of Hinks and introduce herself. But what if

the people seemed as strange and unreal as the town seemed? No, she wanted to get the town under control, first.

The Sporting Emporium, Toggery Bill's, Moss's Photograph Studio, the Craterian Theatre, the Union Building. They were still there. The signs were no doubt different. Modernized. Some of the exteriors had been remodeled. But this was to be expected; this was not what was wrong. It was the whole effect which seemed elusive, mocking, as if it were somehow just out of focus.

She could visit Mrs. McKittrick. There it was, this half-formed impulse, translated into thought. She could visit Mrs. McKittrick, as a kind of preparation for seeing Honey, after so many years. In this way she could feel herself into the situation again; warm up, so to speak, get over this feeling of strangeness.

She knew, from Joseph, that Mrs. McKittrick was a bit senile, poor thing, but they had always got on well together, better even than Mrs. McKittrick had got on with her own daughter. Of course, she could be a bit of a bore. She was devious, tyrannical, but these traits came with her virtues; she had left her mark, not just on her, but on everyone who, in those days, had accepted her hospitality. She had created a "milieu," a "salon," if you could apply such a word to Norton. She certainly ought to visit her, in any case. It would be wrong not to. And she felt certain if there were anyone Mrs. McKittrick would welcome it would be she.

She walked past the Quik-Bite Cafe; it did not occur to her that this was the old Cozy Nook. Something was wrong, but she did not know what. She crossed the bridge. At the further end she stopped, and looked down. How many times she had stood on this bridge with the Trio and looked down and talked. But, until now, she had evidently not really looked; this algae-swarming, green trickle, which was Cold Creek in the summer, might have been the Tiber or the Ganges, so strange and foreign it seemed.

But on the other side of the bridge was the Lower Hill. She began to walk more rapidly. She knew exactly where she was going. How foolish she was, she had meant to go there all along, it was exactly the right thing for her to do.

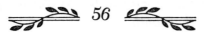

56

SUSANNA FINISHED HER VISIT with her mother early on purpose; she promised to come back after lunch. Now she had an hour before the Reunion; she asked the cabdriver to drop her off in town. She walked down Main Street toward the Lower Hill. Walking like this, through Norton, where few people recognized her anymore, was the closest Susanna ever came to sensuality. She felt like one of the princes in the *Arabian Nights* who wandered through Bagdad in disguise, free to observe and have adventures, unencumbered by his identity.

The town had spread out. There was a new supermarket and shopping center out on the highway. The downtown district was no longer the focal point; it had lost its sense of vitality. This pleased Susanna. It was as if it had stood still just for her, that she might more easily record what changes there were. As she walked, she made mental notes which would go into her notebook upon her return.

It is pear-packing season; the town is more bustling than usual; there are dark-skinned, Mexican faces, among the crowd, which will disappear by the end of the month.

Gidol's Furniture Store, now empty building. Norton Art Club having its show there. Oil painting of Possum Bridge by Dr. Vincent Holbrook in window. Good composition, muddy colors. Congratulations, Vince!

Rialto Theatre's old neo-Venetian facade replaced by modern one. Too bad Bennet Tidewater could not have rummaged among the debris.

New public swimming pool in park, filled with screaming children.

Natatorium long gone.

Old men, like Greek chorus, still sitting on benches on courthouse lawn.

Same old mountains, obscured, now, by haze from the sun.

"Something is going to happen," said Bennet Tidewater.

The Cozy Nook Cafe, now known as the Quik-Bite. We met after movies here, huddled in a booth, wiping away tears, suppressing laughter. "I am madly, madly, in love with Cary Grant," said Janet, insincerely.

A jet plane divided the sky, leaving a trail of white mist. Susanna crossed the bridge that led to the Lower Hill.

57

WHAT ARE HONEY and Joseph thinking of, wondered Janet, how could they have let it happen? The McKittrick house, this once gracious home, looked, from the outside, like a slum. Anger seized her, if she lived here, if Mrs. McKittrick were her mother, she would not have permitted this to occur. She had too much respect for the past, too many memories — It was an outrage against her memories; it was as if the decay were personally directed at her.

You see, the house seemed to say, this is what happens to Personality and Charm. They are as ephemeral as Love and Beauty —

A pickup truck with the words, BOB BLAIR, HANDYMAN, written on the side of it, was parked in the street.

Janet unfastened the wire which held the horrid gate and walked up the weed-choked path to the sagging porch steps. Her high heels made a funny, hollow noise, a kind of echo, as she crossed the porch to the front door. She felt a sudden faintness.

She stopped for a moment to compose herself. From inside the house she could hear voices; then a man's laughter. She must have company, Janet thought. She put out her hand and rang the bell. The bell reverberated inside the house; the voices ceased. Now all was quiet. But no one came. She rang the bell, again. Again, silence. Her uneasiness increased. She glanced at the window which she knew led to Dr. McKittrick's den. The curtains on the window seemed to sway slightly; briefly, she discerned an old woman's face. The eyes of this face met hers coldly, then the curtains fell back again into place; the face vanished.

Oh, God, she thought. Her head felt giddy. She ran back to the path. Then she stopped, and once more looked back at the house. From where she stood, she could no longer see the den window. She glanced upwards. Now the curtains on the window of Honey's room parted, and another face peered out. Susanna! It was Susanna's face she saw. No, she must be mad, she must be absolutely mad!

"You give in to your emotions too much," Dr. Kedy had said. "You must learn to discipline them."

Of course, it could not be Susanna! With a tremendous force of will she made herself look again. The window stared down blankly, the curtains drawn. She turned, and opened the gate. When she reached the sidewalk, she began to run.

 58

SUSANNA WALKED PAST the McKittrick house. A truck was parked in front; it said BOB BLAIR, HANDYMAN on its door. The curtains of the house were drawn, the gate was shut. She walked briskly on, then turned into the walk of the Norton Dental Clinic, which had once been her home. Instead of entering the Clinic, she walked around it to the back. The backyard was all paved now, and landscaped with planters filled with flowers and a table and benches. No doubt the employees ate their lunch here on warm days. She walked through this patio to the alley, which ran behind the house. From the alley she walked through the McKittrick garage, which now contained no car, and emerged into the McKittrick backyard.

Dead rose bushes covered a rectangular area where the pool had been. The grass was long, the garden overgrown.

She makes funny little clumping steps. Her heels are too high, and they sink down in the grass. The tray is awkward. Arthur follows her. She talks to Arthur on the way.

She picked up a piece of wood from the ground — a small, thin stick. She climbed the back steps, stepping over a box of groceries. With the stick, she undid the old metal latch and quietly slipped into the house.

She walked through the back porch to the kitchen. The kitchen looked like a discarded set for an historical B movie. The walls were papered with a faded French Provincial scene — peasants and their carts and dogs — and decorated with dusty copper pans. A shriveled salami and a moldy Italian cheese hung from the ceiling. There was a dry sink, an herb cupboard and a round pine table. An embroidered sampler over the stove said HOME. The counters and tables were bare. She walked over to the refrigerator and opened it. It was empty except for a half-eaten can of tuna fish, and bottles of beer.

From the kitchen she entered the dining room. The sound of the TV was louder in here. She heard a man's hearty laughter. Bob Blair, handyman, she thought. If he found her here she would say she had knocked and no one had answered and she had become concerned.

The dining table was set for six guests. The best china was out — white with gold rims. Green goblets stood at each place. The centerpiece was an old decoration, consisting of tiny gold-leafed apples. Honey's engagement party centerpiece. Green and gold. She ran a finger over one of the gold apples, leaving a smear in the layer of dust which coated it.

On the sideboard stood a dazzling array of silver, recently polished. She picked up a baroque silver sugar tongs, which lay beside the sugar bowl, and slipped it into the pocket of her coat. She didn't own a nice sugar tongs like this.

Bob Blair, handyman's, voice was louder, now. She could make out one word, "Althea." She slipped into the hall and tiptoed up the stairs.

She stood for a moment in the master bedroom which was stripped, except for the double bed and a rug. Mrs. McKittrick, she thought, must sleep downstairs in the old maid's room.

I saw Dr. McKittrick naked, dancing a sailor's hornpipe, while Mrs. McKittrick clapped her hands.

From here she wandered into Honey's room. It looked exactly as if Honey had left it yesterday.

There were still Godey prints on the pale blue walls, old dance programs stuck into the mirror of the flounced dressing table, photographs of old boyfriends on the tabletop. One, in a small silver frame, was a colored photograph of Jack Parsons in his navy uniform. He was staring straight ahead, with crew cut and straight chin and square shoulders — his eyes too blue, his lips too red, looking more young and earnest than like a Mysterious Stranger.

She opened the closet door, and took a quick inventory. Two old formals, one pale green, one pink — she remembered both; a fluffy white petticoat, a cardboard box filled with old sweaters, a tennis racket, an ironing board, a small portable sewing machine and a pile of yearbooks from Norton High.

Suddenly, a doorbell sounded throughout the house. She tiptoed to the front window, which looked down on the front porch. The doorbell sounded again. She pushed the ruffled curtain back, and looked. In a few moments a figure emerged from the porch and walked hastily out of the gate, and turned toward town. It was Janet!

She went back to the dressing table, and picked up the framed photograph of Jack Parsons and slipped this into her coat pocket, too. Then she tiptoed down the stairs, again, and out of the house.

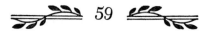 59

"WELL, HERE WE ARE, the Trio, together at last," said Janet, as she had planned to say. "If Honey had not been late, it would not have seemed right."

"Am I late?" said Honey, breathlessly. She looked pretty and disheveled and middle-aged, not at all how Janet had imagined she would look, which was unsettling.

"She is not late, we were early," said Susanna.

The three ladies, once so similar in dress and manner — now, quite different — were standing in the foyer of the Norton Country Club beside a glass case of golf trophies. Chic Janet, eccentric Susanna, and dowdy Honey. If there were anything in common in their appearance, it was that none of them was quite suitably attired for the setting and occasion.

Janet, in a bold black and white checked suit and patent leather accessories, looked too fashionable, as if she were going to model in a style show. Susanna, with her pale braids wrapped about her head, and her pale shapeless dress, which was too long, her sensible shoes and her sensible brown leather bag, looked as if she were going to play a walk-on part in a high school play. Honey still wore her now-graying hair like Brenda Diana Duff Frazier; her blue cotton dress was too bouffant; her blue and white spectator pumps were not quite clean; in one hand she carried a small dingy white purse and her white string gloves rolled up into a ball.

Yet, despite their differences and the oddity of their appearance, or — perhaps because of this — an air of distinction hung over the threesome. They had the sort of distinction that aging, forgotten celebrities, old Follies girls or Miss Americas who come together for a reunion, possess. Their past had been a glamorous one and they were meeting to honor it.

"I suppose we should kiss," said Honey vaguely, and made a clumsy, blind movement toward Janet.

"The Trio never kissed," said Susanna quickly.

"We weren't that type, thank heavens," said Janet. "Of course, I would kiss men. I would kiss Joseph, for example. It was our mothers who kissed women."

Honey laughed. "I wasn't sure, I forget so much, nowadays. Still, between the two, I do prefer to kiss men."

"I don't believe I kiss anyone at all," said Susanna. "I suppose I have a forbidding aspect when it comes to kissing."

"Not so much forbidding as self-contained. I have always admired your aspect," said Janet.

"But, anyway, here we are," said Honey, "together at last. Of course, I've seen Susanna, when she visits her mother. But Janet — you're so elegant and citified!"

Janet, who had prepared her toilet more meticulously than she would have for Joseph, wished she had not, quite; perhaps she looked too planned, too contrived. To make up for her doubts, she took a severe tone with Honey. "But why haven't I seen you, Honey? Sometimes it's made me very cross. I'm sure Joseph has invited you to come to San Francisco with him!" And if you had come, she would liked to have added, things would not have gotten so out of hand.

"Of course he has. Numerous times. But poor Joseph doesn't understand that you just don't pick up and leave town when you have two little girls —"

"You're not that tied down to domestic life, for heaven's sakes?" asked Janet, in a scolding tone.

Honey gave a little apologetic smile. "Oh, Janet, you know how I've always found a rut and stayed in it," she said. This was a lie, but a charming and unself-conscious one, which had a relaxing effect on everyone. "Probably the girls could do without me," she said, "and I just refuse to recognize it. I've reserved a table for us on the terrace, we don't need to hold our Reunion in the hall."

Janet and Susanna followed Honey through the vestibule and out to the terrace. The terrace was filled with other lunchers, mostly women, a few men. Some of them waved or nodded to Honey. A murmur of low voices filled the balmy air.

"I have a table for us in the corner, where we won't be bothered, where we can gossip to our heart's content," Honey said.

A hostess met them and led them to the table. It was almost on the edge of the golf course. The fairways stretched away into woods; the greens, dotted with miniature figures and tiny red flags, had the texture of velvet, the color of emeralds. The mountains, surrounding the course, were enveloped in a gentle summer haze. A gentleman in shorts and cap was teeing off just below them. From around a corner came the noise of the swimming pool — of children shouting and splashing, and bouncing on the diving board.

"It's so lovely, it's like a dream," said Janet. "I do miss the Norton summers. I must admit that."

"It's like a dream, our being here together," Honey said. "The Trio! All for one and one for all! Wasn't that our motto?"

"We had no motto," Susanna said.

"Just the same we are here, which is a kind of victory," said Janet.

"Of mind over matter," said Honey, dreamily.

"No, not *over* matter, because we are here, materially," Susanna said.

Janet opened her purse. She took out her dark glasses and put them on. Then she took out a package of cigarettes and offered them around. Susanna accepted one, holding it and looking at it curiously for a moment, then putting it squarely between her lips so Janet could light it. She took funny little short puffs — the puffs of a nonsmoker — as if she were participating in some strange foreign rite, because the propriety of the moment demanded it. Honey declined one, saying modestly that she had given up smoking for Lent this year, and had not taken it up, again.

"I remember when they built this club. One of the first times we came here was after Honey's wedding," said Janet.

"Tell me about it," said Honey, eagerly.

"We were all in a state of shock — Buzzy had drunk too much champagne and got sick."

"It was just as shocking having to go away," Honey said. "I felt as if I were missing the party."

"It was a beautiful wedding," said Janet. "You and Jack Parsons were the most handsome couple I have ever seen."

"I came across a snapshot of him the other day," said Honey. "He didn't look handsome, exactly. He looked old-fashioned. I suppose it was his haircut. His ears stuck out."

"He was handsome in his time," Susanna said.

In the sunlight Janet noticed that Honey's hair was quite gray. "You're getting gray," she burst out. "You can do something about it, you know."

"I suppose I ought to, but it seems like so much trouble."

"Nothing is too much trouble for a man." Janet laughed, a rather high-pitched laugh. "Isn't it marvelous how full of advice I can be on this subject when I have failed myself?"

"Failed?" cried Honey. "Why, Janet, think what you've accomplished compared to me! A career! The very thought of it fills me with awe."

The gentleman on the ninth tee had moved on. Two older ladies, dressed in white, stood in his place, taking turns teeing off. The tables on the terrace were all filled, now; the murmur of voices, the noise from the pool blended harmoniously into a cacophony of sweet sound. A kind of longing seized Janet — it arose from a memory of her youth in which the future had seemed filled with mysterious delights.

"Remember when we used to play Kick the Can and Sardine at your house, Honey?" she said. "Remember those evenings?" She had never been able to explain their magic to Dr. Kedy. Now she needed to have it verified by the others.

"Of course I do," said Honey. "Wasn't I madly in love with Teddy Lyons then?"

"Poor Buzzy," said Janet.

"Why 'poor Buzzy?' " said Honey.

"Because he always liked you, he was always loyal."

"Poor Vince, in that case," Honey said.

"But why 'poor Vince?' "

"He was in love with you," said Honey. "Really, you ought to have married him, Janet. Didn't you always want to marry a doctor?"

"You act as if I had the opportunity," Janet said. The dream had vanished; Dr. Kedy, no doubt, was correct in doubting the existence of such a time.

"But of course you did!"

"He liked *you*, Honey."

"Well, I didn't mean he didn't like me, but he liked you best."

"He admired your good bony structure," said Susanna. "Doctors are that way. They like finely built, healthy, sturdy girls for breeding purposes."

"Like the New Girl, Stella Marsh?"

"Stella has had six babies," said Honey.

"My God," said Janet, "can you imagine me doing that?"

"Well, of course I could, Jan. You could just never imagine yourself," Honey said.

"Anyhow, he liked Honey," said Janet.

"If he did, I never knew it," Honey said.

"Well, I suppose we could call him up and ask him whom he liked?" Janet said.

" 'Vince, was it Janet or Honey you preferred?' " said Susanna.

" 'It was Janet,' " said Honey. " 'I always admired her fine bony structure.' "

" 'Well, we just wondered, thank you very much,' " said Susanna.

"Please," said Janet, "I can't stand it. We are getting too loud."

A waitress approached them across the terrace. "It's Evajean," said Honey.

"Do we know her?" said Janet.

"Evajean Watkins?" said Honey.

"Of course we know her, her maiden name was Treece," Susanna said.

"I do not believe in women changing their names, it makes it so difficult," Janet said. She had once considered taking legal action to recover her maiden name, for, being childless, why should she go through life with the name of a man she hated; on the other hand, she had not cared much for her father, either; she had thought it was her mother, but it was her father, it turned out, so she had not bothered with the legal action, after all.

"She was the Poor Girl," Susanna said.

"What a dreadful thing to have called her, what snobs we must have been," said Janet.

"But it was what we called her," said Susanna.

"She could not have been any poorer than I was," Janet said.

"It was a question of background," said Susanna.

Evajean Watkins, née Treece, approached their table now. "What is this, girls, a Reunion?" she said cheerfully.

"Susanna is here to visit her mother and Janet is here on business," Honey said.

"The Trio, we used to call you the Trio," said Evajean.

"We must have seemed — awfully — clannish," said Janet.

"You were best friends," said Evajean. "That's how it goes." She stood smiling down at the Trio in a maternal kind of way. "Time flies, don't it?" she said. "Janet is a career girl, and Susanna is a teacher. I know all about you. Mrs. McKittrick keeps me in touch."

Janet felt a stab of envy. "Oh, do you see Honey's mother?" she asked lightly.

"I try to call on her at least once a month. She was always so good to me, when I was a kid. I know how busy Honey is with her family, and anyway I'm terribly fond of her. We play gin rummy or watch TV together. She really is a remarkable old lady. So keen."

"Do you have a family?" said Susanna.

"I'm a grandmother," said Evajean. "I have the cutest baby grandson you've ever seen." She reached in the pocket of her uniform and took out her wallet; from this she extracted a photograph and passed it around.

Susanna studied it carefully; Janet and Honey uttered little appreciative cries.

"But you certainly don't look like a grandmother," said Janet to Evajean.

"Time flies," said Evajean. "You girls look real good, too. Are you going to have a drink?"

Janet and Susanna ordered gin and tonics; Honey, a sherry.

"She must have loathed us," said Janet, after Evajean left. "We must have been loathsome."

Honey said, "Oh? Why?"

"We were so insular, so mean. Girls, nowadays, have broader interests. They aren't so narrow."

Susanna said, "Bennet Tidewater said we were monsters."

Honey said, "Did he say that?"

"All we did was gossip and think about sex," said Janet.

"I'm sure I'd do the same thing all over again," Honey said, with a giggle.

"We went to movies," Susanna said.

"Honey was always late," said Janet. "She always missed *The March of Time*."

"You were in love with Cary Grant," said Susanna to Janet.

"Please," said Janet. "There are some things, Susanna, you should not remind people of."

"What is the matter with Cary Grant?" said Honey.

"I can't bear to even discuss it," cried Janet. She took out her cigarettes again. Susanna declined one. Janet decided it was time to say what she had planned to say. "If a thing like growing up in Norton happens to you, you cannot escape it, it stays with you all of your life."

"Why should you want to escape it?" said Honey, earnestly.

"I think I know what Janet means," said Susanna. She knew it was not what Janet meant, but wanting to say what she had planned to say, she took this opportunity. "When I had my girls in Rome last summer," she said, "I was standing on the Spanish Steps, the girls were chatting with some American college boys sitting around the fountain. There I was, standing on the Spanish Steps, and it occurred to me that if someone had asked me the name of the building which used to be at Fourth and Main in Norton, Oregon, and from which we watched the Armistice Day parades, I could have told him, the Union Building, and I could also have told him the name of the man who owned the building, Mr. Brewer, and how he was killed in an automobile accident on the Old Stage Road and how his wife remarried the man who owned the Sporting Emporium where there was the big moose head on the wall which said KILLED BY JIM ROGERS under it, and how, when I was a child, the moose head used to frighten me, but perhaps that is too subjective a comment, and I could also have told him that Jim Rogers' daughter worked at the Fountain of Beauty and was wall-eyed, and so you see, there I was standing on the Spanish Steps, except that, at that moment, I was also connected to Norton, so in a way, Norton had everything to do with the Spanish Steps, as Janet has pointed out."

"If I have pointed that out," said Janet, "it was quite unintentional, as it was not what I meant to point out at all."

"Sorry," said Susanna.

"What I meant to point out had nothing to do with Armistice Day parades or Sporting Emporiums or moose heads. Nothing at all. Though, now that you have brought them up, I should like to say that your moose head is undoubtedly a phallic symbol. You were frightened by it as a child. Doesn't that seem to have symbolic meaning? You have to stop thinking in terms of moose heads and think what moose heads represent."

"Perhaps it is a phallic symbol, but it is also and undeniably a moose head, we are certain of that," said Susanna.

"Moreover, if you don't mind — Spanish *Steps*," said Janet. "Steps are a well-known sex symbol. Looking at Spanish Steps and thinking of moose heads is too much, Susanna."

"But I did not say I thought of moose heads. As a matter of fact, I did not think of them. I merely said that if someone had asked me the name of the building at Fourth and Main in Norton, I could have supplied it, as well as other pertinent information regarding it."

"Did someone ask you?" said Honey.

"Of course no one asked her," said Janet.

Susanna, who had overcome all tendencies toward fantasy by the study of facts, experienced a sudden relapse. "Imagine my standing on the Spanish Steps and a gentleman, an Italian gentleman, with a mustache and a white suit, coming up to me, and saying —"

" 'Signora,' " continued Janet, " 'would you please supply me with the name of the building at

Fourth and Main in Norton, Oregon?' And, of course, Susanna would! Without blinking an eye!"

"Yes, I can see you, Susanna — just calmly supplying the name," Honey said. "And then you would tell him about the moose head. Oh, I can see it all!"

"We are being much too silly, people are looking at us, we must have more dignity," Janet said.

"Remember you are a Queen, and everyone else is your subject," said Honey, and went off into a fit of laughter. "I really think I ought to have ordered a gin and tonic, I can't bear it!" she cried.

"Gin is full of calories and causes pimples," Susanna said.

"All I was saying, before Susanna tried to interpret what I was saying, is that one can't escape one's past."

"But why should you want to escape it?" said Honey, brushing away the tears.

"People differ," said Janet, severely. "I shouldn't expect you, Honey, to feel the same way."

"Janet means your Past was a glorious one," said Susanna.

"You were the prettiest girl in town," said Janet.

A dreamy look came over Honey's eyes. She did not try to defend herself against this accusation.

"Still, it is not easy to be beautiful," said Susanna. "I am quoting Bennet Tidewater."

"Did he say that?" said Honey, eagerly.

"Oh, please, not him," begged Janet. "Tell me about your mother," she said to Honey. It seemed to her, suddenly, that what had occurred this morning was not real, had not happened. The town had affected her strangely; her nerves had been bad. The voices and laughter she had heard were probably from the television set; Mrs. McKittrick, no doubt, was deaf; the faces at the window were a product of her own hysteria. "I would like to visit her," she said, but her voice quavered; she felt Susanna's sharp gaze.

"I don't think it would matter much if you did," said Honey. "Evajean was just being kind. She is in her dotage."

"But for old time's sake!"

"I have never understood doing something for Time," said Honey. "But perhaps that is because I am a monster."

"I am beginning to think you are, Honey McKittrick! How would you feel if your daughters never visited you?" Had it happened, or had it not happened, thought Janet. She would never know.

"If I am like my mother," said Honey, "I would not care."

"I am shocked," said Janet, sincerely.

"Bennet Tidewater said Honey was the most monstrous," Susanna said.

Honey laughed.

"Is there anything Bennet Tidewater didn't comment on?" cried Janet.

"He thought you were the least monstrous, Janet, because you were the most burdened by a sense of guilt," Susanna said.

"But that is exactly what I've been spending years and every extra penny to get rid of," Janet cried.

"And yet you are still shocked when others don't feel guilty."

"Joseph is, too," said Honey. "He is shocked because I don't visit my mother."

"Your mother did so much for us in the old days," Janet said.

"But that was in the old days," said Honey, serenely.

"How can you say, but that was in the old days, as if — as if they are gone forever, as if they don't matter at all!"

Evajean arrived with the drinks. "Here are the menus, girls," she said. "We're out of stroganoff. The Crab Louis looks good today. Now you better toast the Trio, for old time's sake."

"Honey does not believe in doing things for old time's sake," said Janet.

"Honey, I'm ashamed of you. The Trio was an institution," said Evajean with flat conviction.

"Honey is not burdened by false sentimentality," said Susanna, lightly.

"Everyone knew about the Trio," said Evajean. "Now, pick up your glasses, girls."

Honey smiled. They picked up their glasses. "To the Trio!" Evajean cried.

"To the Trio," they all said, softly, and drank.

"Well, now, that's better! I'm going to bring you the Crab Louis, unless anyone objects," said Evajean.

No one objected. She left, and they sighed with relief.

"She has forgotten she tried to break us up," said Janet. "She tried to worm her way into Honey's affections. I remember now."

"Only because we were an entity worth worming into," said Susanna.

"I really don't like Crab Louis," Janet said.

"She assumes the Trio all eat alike," said Susanna.

"She is having her revenge," said Janet. "She will probably put poison in it. Well, I wouldn't blame her. We must have been awful."

"Oh, I don't think we were that bad," Honey said.

"Henny thought we were," said Janet.

"Who was Henny?" said Honey.

"Miss Louise Henderson, the bitch."

"Didn't we used to go to her apartment and read poetry and eat cookies?"

"That was in our Lesbian stage," said Janet.

"Oh, Jan, we were never that!" Honey said.

"Honey, you are raising two daughters. You ought to be more realistic. Of course we went through a Lesbian stage. Normal girls do. That was what made us so idealistic about the Trio."

"Now, *I'm* shocked, Jan!" cried Honey. "You mean the Trio was just a bunch of Lesbians?"

"That doesn't mean it was bad, Honey. Not if you outgrow it. My trouble is, it took me too long."

"To say we were Lesbians is no more or no less of the truth, whatever the truth may be, than to say we all had two legs and two arms. It does not, I think, explain the Trio," Susanna said.

"Well, thank God for that," said Honey.

"There was a young man who wanted to kill you," said Susanna to Honey. "He worked at a service station, and became distraught when you wanted to drop him."

"Did he really want to kill me?" Honey gave a delighted little shudder.

"He sent you menacing notes, as I recall. Do you remember his name?" said Susanna.

"Let me see — Oh, Susanna, I'm afraid I don't."

"Then tell us about Harry Nakamura," said Susanna.

"He's the girls' orthodontist, and president of the Chamber of Commerce," Honey said.

"Tell us about Buzzy," said Janet.

"Buzzy is over all the time, when he's not in Washington. He's practically a member of our family. The girls adore him."

"And he really does manage?" said Susanna.

"Oh, my, yes."

"I can't even bear to think about it," Janet cried.

"That's because you don't see him, you only know the bad part," said Honey.

Evajean brought the salads.

"And now," said Honey, picking up her fork, "I want to know all about you two. Joseph will ask me. Since we only write at Christmas time, you'll have to fill me in. Let's begin with you, Susanna."

"I shall try not to bore you with too long an account of an uneventful but satisfying existence," Susanna said. "I shall be going to Europe again this summer with a group of girls. We shall tour England and the Scandinavian countries. My life is very ordered, very tidy. I have no lovers. I believe I am reasonably content." She smiled an elfin, spinsterish smile, and began to eat.

"But your writing, Susanna," said Honey. "We've always been waiting for that Great American novel. Have you given that up?"

Susanna put her fork down. "I think," she said,

slowly, "that the nicest thing that ever happened to me was when I realized, one day, that I had no talent."

"Oh, Susanna!" cried Honey. "You were on the *Modoc,* and on the *Emerald* in college. How can you say such a thing?"

"Because it is true," said Susanna. "Bennet Tidewater tried to tell me, but I was not able to listen, then. I wanted, I suppose, to somehow make permanent all the interesting things I saw and heard. Perhaps my nature is somewhat limited, but now I am quite content with seeing and hearing them. Perhaps one of the girls I teach will do better. That would be quite enough for me." She resumed her meal.

"I don't believe you, Susanna. You're being much too modest. But now let's hear from Jan. Do you have a special beau, Jan, dear?"

Janet thought for a moment — suppose she were to say, "Yes, there is one, your husband?"

"Yes, there is one," she said, "an architect."

"Oh, Jan, does he want to marry you?"

"Yes," she said. If things had worked out just a bit differently, what she was telling Honey would be true. "But, there are — problems," she said. "I'm seeing my psychiatrist about it."

"My goodness, what does he say?"

"It's a she, and she says nothing."

"And you pay — for that?"

"I have to work it out, myself. She only guides me. When one has been burnt once, one is very careful."

"This architect — are you in love with him, Jan?"

"In love? It's so hard to know, isn't it? I mean, what is love?"

"Oh, Jan!"

"When you're my age, and a divorcée, you lead a sort of fringe existence. All your friends have their hang-ups. My architect is divorced, and one of his children is in a mental institution."

"Oh, Jan!"

"He is an ex-alcoholic."

"Poor, dear Jan!"

"But he's terribly attractive and extremely talented."

"Jan, you must move back to Norton. I know I could find someone suitable for you. There's an awfully nice widower with heaps of money. He's not exactly dashing, but he'd be terribly stable."

"My happily married friends always try to fix me up with someone like that, but it never seems to work. Besides, Honey, I do have my job. Norton is not the world — at least not my world, anymore."

Evajean brought coffee. Susanna said, "Now, Honey, tell us about yourself."

"What shall I tell? I lead such an ordinary life compared to you two."

"Tell us about our namesakes," said Janet.

"Oh, the girls are fine. I hope you'll see them."

"And Joseph —"

"Joseph is fine." Honey picked up her coffee cup, and held it, hesitating, before her mouth. Then she set it down, without tasting the coffee.

"Are you in activities, P.T.A., that sort of thing?" said Janet, urging her on.

"I'm really a dreadful homebody," said Honey.

"Well, there must be something you can say," said Janet, sternly.

"Perhaps there is — I'm not sure I should, though."

"A secret?" said Janet.

A lock of gray hair fell over Honey's eye; she brushed it back, and smiled up at Janet and Susanna. "You might call it that," she said.

"You have to tell us, then. You can't stop now. After all, we are the Trio," said Janet.

"If you weren't the Trio, I wouldn't dream of telling you."

"You're having an affair," said Janet, as a joke.

Honey smiled, again. "You must promise faithfully, cross your hearts, hope to die —?"

They crossed their hearts.

"Yes, I'm having an affair."

"You are what?" cried Janet. Then, quickly controlling herself, she added an arch, "Oh?" After that she said, "With — who?" weakly.

"With whom," corrected Susanna.

"Is it someone we know?" Janet said.

"Or a Mysterious Stranger?" Susanna said.

"Someone you know," said Honey.

"It's Vince, it must be Vince," Janet said.

Honey giggled.

"You have to tell us, now, you can't just stop in the middle, after all we are the Trio."

"He's absolutely, divinely dreamy," said Honey.

"Teddy Lyons is dead," said Janet.

"Nathan Brenner is in Berkeley," said Susanna.

"He isn't Honey's type, anyhow," said Janet.

There was another silence. Then Janet said, "It must be Buzzy." Her voice was incredulous. "Is it Buzzy?"

"Yes, it's Buzzy," laughed Honey.

"I don't believe it. You mean, a *real* affair?"

"What other sort is there?" said Susanna.

"But — how does this fit in with your religion?" said Janet.

"Not awfully well. It's a mortal sin, you see." Her voice sounded faraway.

"And I suppose you just go and confess, and then everything is dandy?"

"Oh, no, Jan. Not at all. You have to be honestly

penitent, and that's the trouble, you see. I *like* having the affair. So at the moment, I have to abstain from the sacraments. I have no other choice."

"But how can you just sit there and say that — so — so calmly," Janet said.

"You made me tell you."

"Well, of course we did," said Susanna.

"But I still don't understand," said Janet. "What is your future? You can't divorce and stay in the church, can you?"

"Heavens, no. I suppose I shall have to give him up eventually. If Bennet Tidewater were alive, I would talk to him."

"Oh, for God's sakes, Bennet Tidewater," Janet said. "What you need, Honey, is a qualified person to discuss your problems with. Isn't there a psychiatrist in Norton?"

"Goodness, no, not in Norton," said Honey.

"Well, then, you must come and visit me and talk to my doctor. Or she would recommend someone to you. You have no idea, Honey, how helpful it would be. You simply must."

"Oh, I couldn't leave Joseph and the girls."

"But you have left Joseph!"

"Of course I haven't left Joseph. I'm merely, at this moment, living in a state of sin. Since I know this, I don't see how a psychiatrist could help me. I probably need a spiritual adviser."

"Have you talked to your — your priest?" said Janet.

"Yes."

"What did he tell you?"

"That I am living in a state of sin."

"How dreadful to think that!" said Janet.

"It is nicer not to have to."

"Susanna, you haven't said a word," said Janet. "What are you thinking?"

"I, too, was wondering what Bennet Tidewater would say. He believed, of course, in the sanctity of the home. He would not have sanctioned divorce."

"Oh, divorce is quite out of the question," Honey said.

"This is incredible," said Janet. She lit another cigarette. Her fingers trembled. "Joseph — does Joseph know?"

"Of course he doesn't."

"And what is Buzzy's point of view?"

"He loves me, but he is quite prepared to give me up. He isn't Catholic, but he understands my position."

"Something must be done," said Janet. "You must let the Trio help you."

"I would be so happy if you could. But Jan, you musn't worry about me. Here we are, the Trio. We'll always be that, anyway, until death."

"Until death?" Janet shivered with distaste. "I forget you're Catholic, sometimes, Honey, until you say things like that."

Honey smiled.

"We must ask for the check," said Susanna. "Mother is expecting me again after lunch, and Janet wants to call on your mother." Her glance fell cryptically on Janet. Then she turned back to Honey. "Perhaps we can drop in late this afternoon and see your girls. We leave on the eight o'clock plane."

"How can we just leave — after Honey has told us this?" Janet said. "I feel as if we should stay and do something."

"There is nothing to do, and it is necessary to leave," Susanna said.

"Oh, it's been so much fun, and much too short," said Honey.

While Honey was signaling Evajean, Susanna turned to Janet. "Tell me one thing, before we disband, did Gerald Kroner have a mustache?" she asked.

"Susanna, what possible difference, and at such a time! No, he did not!"

"Thank you, I was afraid I might forget to ask," Susanna said.

The gentleman who had been on the ninth tee as the Trio sat down to lunch, now appeared, showered, in fresh flannels, holding a gin and tonic in his hand. The tables on the terrace had begun to empty; the noise from the pool seemed louder. Evajean brought the check, which Honey insisted on signing.

"Well, girls, how did it go?" she said to them.

"It was a lovely Reunion," said Honey.

60

"I WASN'T GOING TO CALL YOU, but, oh, Joseph, I couldn't help it. We must have a talk, we must help Honey," said Janet to Joseph, whom she had reached by phone at his office.

"Meet me at the airport at four," said Joseph. "We can fly up to Possum Bridge — there's a landing field, now. We can talk there, no one will see us."

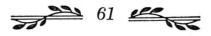 *61*

"TELL ME ABOUT THE TRIO," said Mrs. McKittrick to Evajean.

"Susanna looks like an old maid; Janet is very stylish."

"I saw her through the window," Mrs. McKittrick said. "Stylish is as stylish does, I've always said. I'm surprised she fell for that son-in-law of mine. You don't have to tell me what goes on when he goes to San Francisco. I would have thought she might have had better taste. But when do you suppose Honey will divorce him?"

"Honey is Catholic," Evajean said. "Catholics don't divorce."

"Pooh," said Mrs. McKittrick. "They divorce all the time. You don't have to tell me about Catholics."

"I suppose she could claim they weren't married in the church," said Evajean.

"She'll think of something," Mrs. McKittrick said. "It will work out for Honey, it always has. By the way, Susanna has stolen my sugar tongs."

"Susanna hasn't been to see you," Evajean said.

"She must have been here, because the tongs are gone. She was always a little thief. Crime runs in her family. Shall we watch the 'Today' show, or do you want to play gin rummy?"

"Let's play gin rummy," said Evajean. "I've brought you some beer."

62

THEY HAD DONE WESTMINISTER ABBEY and they had done the Tower and now they were having tea in a small tearoom, when Barby Hall said, "Tell us about the airplane crash, Miss Swope."

"Yes, please, Miss Swope," said Cathy Gregerson.

"The plane was found in the Modoc River," said Susanna. "Joseph somehow missed the landing field, and hit a bridge support, and it catapulted in. It took two days to recover the bodies, two more days to dredge the plane out of the mud. I stayed in Norton with Honey until Congressman Heffelfinger returned from Washington. Bitsy, will you please pass the crumpets around the table? This is only teatime, there will be a supper later on."

"Do you think it was suicide?" said Barby.

"Suicide? How does one know? All we can see are the facts. We do not know the truth. Sometimes, the more I examine the facts, the less I believe they are real, the more they seem to elude me. No, I do not believe the facts are the truth, anymore than the chemical content of our bodies make up a person. Yet that is all I have, at any rate. I find it better not to speculate. It certainly was not suicide in the usual, planned sense, and, if it were, what a dreadful thing to take Janet with him. Still, something was bound to happen. Things could not go on as they were."

"And now Honey will marry Congressman Heffelfinger," said Cathy.

"And they will live happily ever after," said Bitsy, her mouth full of crumpet.

"I do not know if they will, yet it is quite possible that they may."

"But the Trio is no more," said Barby.

"That is a fact, at any rate," Susanna said. "Janet broke up the Trio by her death. Or, you might say that Honey broke it up, by having an affair with Buzzy, which prompted Janet to go for that plane ride with Joseph. Or perhaps I was instrumental, by playing such a passive role. Even Mrs. McKittrick was involved by rejecting Joseph and Janet. Who knows, maybe even Bennet Tidewater was not without influence. One can say all sorts of things, but it will get us nowhere. There is no more Trio. Honey and I are released from that peculiar bondage. When my mother dies, I shall probably never return to Norton. It is the end of the story, so to say that the lovers will live happily ever after is no doubt appropriate, after all. But what is even more appropriate, at the moment, is this poem written by Sir Walter Raleigh, supposedly on the night before his execution in the Tower. I shall ask you to listen quietly as I read it to you.

> *Even such is time, that takes in trust*
> *Our youth, our joys, our all we have,*
> *And pays us but with age and dust;*
> *Who, in the dark and silent grave,*
> *When we have wandered all our ways,*
> *Shuts up the story of our days;*
> *But from which earth, and grave, and dust,*
> *The Lord shall raise me up, I trust.*

"I do not know if his God raised him up," said Susanna, closing the book, and folding her napkin upon it. "I am not equipped with a religious nature, or, if I once had one, it has been suppressed. That speculation is quite beyond me. All I know is that it is a very good poem, and in an odd way, comforting."